The main <...>
was over

"My compliments to the chef," Joy said when they were curled up on the sofa, sipping brandy. "That was a wonderful dinner."

"Compliments? Is that all the chef gets?" Andy teased.

"What else could a chef want besides compliments and empty plates?"

"He might want an after-dinner kiss." Deftly he removed the snifter from her hand. His fingers grazed her skin in the process, setting off fireworks.

"Is that like an after-dinner mint?" she asked breathlessly.

"Better! And what comes after *that* will be even more satisfying...."

Mary Jo Territo grew up in New Jersey and moved to New York City after finishing college. She worked in the theater and later as an editor at Richard Gallen Books before starting to write fiction on her own.

Catch a Rising Star is a delightful, realistic tale that draws strongly on Mary Jo's years as a struggling actress. Broadway's loss is definitely publishing's gain!

Books by Mary Jo Territo

HARLEQUIN TEMPTATION
52–JUST FRIENDS

HARLEQUIN SUPERROMANCE
190–TWO TO TANGO

These books may be available at your local bookseller.

Don't miss any of our special offers. Write to us at the following address for information on our newest releases.

Harlequin Reader Service
901 Fuhrmann Blvd., P.O. Box 1397, Buffalo, NY 14240
Canadian address: P.O. Box 2800, Postal Station A,
5170 Yonge St., Willowdale, Ont. M2N 6J3

Catch a Rising Star

MARY JO TERRITO

Harlequin Books

TORONTO • NEW YORK • LONDON
AMSTERDAM • PARIS • SYDNEY • HAMBURG
STOCKHOLM • ATHENS • TOKYO • MILAN

To Joyce,
with memories of our little dump
on West 46th Street

Published June 1986

ISBN 0-373-25211-0

1

FROM A BACK CORNER of the restaurant, Joy Kingsley eyed the last couple still seated at her station. Weren't they ever going to leave? she wondered irritably. It was after one in the morning. Her shift had started at five, she was dog-tired and to top it off she had an audition the following afternoon. Stifling a yawn, she poured herself the last of the coffee from the glass pot and sat down at a table to sort through the evening's checks.

"Coffee at this hour, Joy? You'll never get to sleep."

"That's the point, Chris," she said to her fellow waitress, also an unemployed actress, as was everyone who waited tables or tended bar in the restaurant.

"Hot date?" Chris asked with the crooked-faced grin that always reminded Joy of a kid in a painting by Norman Rockwell. Chris Owens was one hundred percent American ingenue—a pert strawberry blonde with enormous blue eyes and full rosy cheeks.

"I should be so lucky," Joy answered dryly. "Big audition tomorrow afternoon."

"You're supposed to sleep before auditions—be well rested," Chris counseled. "At least that's what they told me in acting school."

"They lied," Joy joked. "Who can sleep? I don't even know what I'm going to do yet."

"What's it for?"

"I won the Equity lottery. Got a slot at the regional theater auditions." Every year the actors' union sponsored auditions that were attended by directors of regional theaters from all over the country. There were always many more applicants than places, so a lottery system had been devised. Before that people had camped out on the street in front of the Equity offices overnight in order to sign up for a spot.

"You're lucky," Chris said enviously.

"Me and a couple hundred other actors."

"That's not a great attitude, Joy," Chris chided lightly.

"I know, but I always feel this way when I have to do a monologue." Joy screwed an index finger to her temple and grimaced goofily.

Chris laughed and clapped her on the shoulder. "I know exactly what you mean."

"I'd like to know who invented monologues," Joy said testily. "I mean, would anyone audition a concert pianist by asking them to play sixteen bars of the *Moonlight Sonata*?"

"Probably not," Chris said with a knowing chuckle. She fanned the sheaf of checks she had in her hand. "Well, I think I'll hand these in and head off home. Hope you get out of here soon."

"Me, too. G'night," Joy said as she went off.

Chris paused near the kitchen door and then turned back to Joy. "Hey," she called. "Break a leg tomorrow."

Joy gave her a thumbs-up signal and went back to sorting her checks. But it was hard to keep her mind on her work. Four years ago when she'd come to New York, she'd known it was going to be tough. But not this tough. Despite a lot of hard work she was still waiting tables to keep body and soul together between all too infrequent acting jobs. Sometimes it was difficult to hold on to her faith in herself and her talent and keep going.

The last customers were still lingering over their coffee, and she decided to give them two more minutes before presenting the check. The manager didn't like the staff to hurry people, and she'd probably get chewed out if he caught her, but tonight was a special case. A lot of directors with whom she'd been trying unsuccessfully to get an audition were going to be present tomorrow afternoon, and she was going to have to do one heck of a job to make herself stand out from all the competition.

Two minutes later the couple was still engrossed in conversation. Joy toted up the bill and strolled over to the table. "Can I get you folks anything else?" she asked with more cordiality than she felt. When they said no, she put the check on the table and waited. Usually she did something else while the customers fumbled with wallets and figured out her tip, but tonight she hovered over the table, hoping they'd take the hint, pay up and leave.

The man gave her an annoyed look, but then glanced around the restaurant and saw they were the only ones left. "I guess you want to get home," he said, placing some bills on the tray and handing it to her. Joy nodded gratefully and took the check to the cash register. When she returned the man said, "My wife thinks we saw you in *Pie in the Sky*, that revue down at the Village Gate last year."

"You sure did," she said, placing the change on the table. Usually she got a kick out of being recognized, but she was too pooped and too anxious to get home to do much more than smile thinly.

"We really enjoyed it," the woman enthused.

"Thank you," Joy said, managing a small bow. "Thank you very much." The woman seemed about to say something else, but Joy headed her off. "I really hate to rush you, but I've got a big audition tomorrow and I'd—"

The man held up his hand. "It is late," he said, standing to help his wife into her coat.

"Thanks a lot." She was itching to grab her tip, clear the table and close out her station in record time, but she stood by politely as the couple bundled up against the winter wind. "I really appreciate it." As soon as they had both taken a step toward the door, she started snatching the coffee cups, dessert plates and cutlery off the table.

Fifteen minutes later she dashed out onto Forty-second Street. A fierce gust of icy wind stung her face and eyes, but it felt good after the smoky, stuffy air inside the restaurant. Luckily, home was just around the corner in the same apartment tower that housed the café on its ground floor. Joy nipped down Ninth Avenue and into the building lobby. This tower, and an identical one behind it on Tenth Avenue, collectively known as Manhattan Plaza, provided subsidized housing for performing artists. Joy had moved into her studio apartment only a couple of months before, having worked her way up from the bottom of the long waiting list.

She nodded to the night guard at the desk as she went through the lobby to the elevator banks. In seconds she was on the thirty-eighth floor, letting herself into her apartment. As usual she was irresistibly drawn to the spectacular view from her window. No matter how long she lived here, she knew she'd never tire of the ever-changing show. It was better than a free lifetime pass to the movies. Beneath her the city loomed large and lusty, a living thing, more exciting, enticing, forbidding and frightening than anything ever dreamed up in Hollywood.

The streets and buildings were brightly lit, but the sky above was a dull blue-gray, as if watching over a city that never slept had tired it. Every night Joy looked for stars to wish on, as she had as a child. But they were hard to find; they seemed to be hiding, unwilling to waste their energy competing with the show below. She scanned the sky until she found a small twinkling star. Gazing at it steadily, she wished simply for a well-lighted path that would lead her safely through the next day. She had long ago given up asking for specifics— no more sweaters like her sister Hildy's or A's in algebra. Would that life were still that uncomplicated, she thought wistfully as she lowered the blinds and shut out the city and the sky.

Joy pulled off her black bow tie, stripped away her now grubby white blouse and black trousers and slipped her long, lean body into a comfortable sweat suit. She twisted her abundant chestnut hair into a knot on top of her head and secured it with a large tortoise-shell barrette.

To put the day behind her and get into a receptive frame of mind, she spread her exercise mat on the floor and lay down on it. She let her arms flop at her sides as she performed a relaxation exercise, using her mind to release the tension in every part of her body. After about ten minutes, when she felt calm and energized, she stood up and began to work.

First she imagined herself in the theater where she would be auditioning the following afternoon. She peopled the audience with friendly faces, brought to mind the specific imaginary circumstances she had created for one of her monologues and began to act it. She stopped after the first two sentences, feeling phony and unconnected to the material. She tried again and again, but got no farther. Quelling her rising irritation, she switched to another piece.

She worked for an hour, pulling out all the tricks she'd learned in her acting classes, trying different approaches to all four of her pieces, but she succeeded only in frustrating herself. Finally she flung down the scarf she was using for a prop. "I hate giving monologues," she raged. "It's dumb and stupid—just like I said to Chris before."

As she quieted down, she recognized the first flash of genuine emotion she'd had since she'd started rehearsing. *If you've got it, use it,* her acting teachers always advised, so she grabbed a pad and pencil from her desk and started scribbling at a furious rate.

Dawn was poking its nose through the slats of her window blinds when she finished writing her anti-monologue monologue. By nine o'clock she'd worked her way through an entire pot of coffee, but she had created an audition piece that, if nothing else, was unique, and demonstrated her best acting qualities— directness, a passion that was deeply felt but intelligent and controlled, and a dry, ironic sense of humor.

Exhausted, Joy headed for the shower, washed and dried her hair and fixed herself a hearty breakfast. This refreshed her, but her eyes were still drooping. Bed was tempting, but she was too tired to risk getting too comfortable. If she did, she was liable to sleep through her audition time, so she set her alarm for noon, curled up on the love seat and closed her eyes.

HAIR FLYING BEHIND HER, Joy bounded down Forty-third Street, dashed up Eighth Avenue and rounded the corner onto Forty-sixth Street. She dodged a pair of stagehands carrying a spotlight, ran interference through a group of matrons gawking at a larger-than-life-size cast photo outside a theater and ducked down a dark alleyway, swearing at herself all the while. She should never have taken that nap. She sprinted to the end of the alley, stopped in front of the door to catch her breath and then opened the stage door of the theater.

Inside, an audition monitor was seated at a small table, looking tired and hassled. She gave him her name, and he looked at her sourly as he checked her off his list. "You were supposed to be here at least fifteen minutes before your audition time. The rules set out by the union were very clear," he admonished.

"I'm terribly sorry," Joy said, and gave him an apologetic smile. "I was detained—"

"Spare me," he said wearily, and began to reel off the audition procedure in a monotone. "The stage manager will call your name, lead you onstage, announce your name and selection to the auditioners. If you go over three minutes and fifteen seconds, you'll be interrupted." He handed her an index card. "Print your name and the title and author of your piece on this and give it to the stage manager." Joy filled out the card and hurried down the hall to the backstage area.

There was a time when she'd have been annoyed by such brusque treatment, but now she knew it wasn't worth her energy to get upset about it. The guy at the door had probably been sitting at that desk for the past day and a half, saying the same thing over and over, soothing tempers and egos, trying to keep the auditions running smoothly. He might just as easily have been pleasant and helpful, but he wasn't, and there was nothing she could do about it. Over the years she had schooled herself to ignore the frequent breaches of manners and concentrate on what was important—the audition itself.

The backstage area was littered with waiting actors and actresses, pacing, sitting stiffly on folding metal chairs, leaning casually against a wall or prop table, or performing the various disciplines—yoga, self-hypnosis, special breathing or stretching exercises— they hoped would curb or eliminate preaudition jitters. No one said a word, but several pairs of lips were moving, going over material one more time or saying a final silent prayer.

Joy identified the stage manager by the large stopwatch that dangled conspicuously from a bright red ribbon around her neck. The woman took her index card and quickly glanced at it. Keeping one eye on her stopwatch, she checked Joy's name off her list and whispered, "You're supposed to be next. Know the drill?" Joy said she did. "If you want to catch your breath, I'll let one more person go ahead of you, but if you're ready. . ."

"I'm ready," Joy declared softly but firmly. She wanted to get on the stage before she chickened out and chucked the new monologue. The haste with which she'd left her apartment hadn't left much time for thinking, but the inevitable second thoughts were assailing her full force now. She was taking an enormous risk; her monologue could very well offend more people than it impressed.

Her hands shook slightly as she stripped off her jacket and scarf and deposited them on an empty folding chair. Quickly she took a comb and a small pot of lip gloss from her purse, smoothed a few strands of hair, spread a thin layer of gloss on her lips and tossed the implements back into her purse. Considering she'd dressed in five minutes, she didn't look too bad. Her freshly washed hair fell in thick lustrous waves; her simple makeup—light foundation to protect her sensitive skin from city pollution, mascara and a daub of gray shadow to accentuate her dark, expressive eyes, a few strokes of tawny blusher on her high cheekbones and the coating of colorless gloss—suited her casual attire.

The next two minutes seemed longer than forever to Joy. To help pass the time and quell her nerves, she stretched her arms over her head and bent from side to side a few times. Her palms were disconcertingly damp so she rubbed them hard on the sides of her black jersey harem-style trousers. She fidgeted with the drape of her roomy deep violet sweater and wriggled her toes in her supple calf-height black boots. But she couldn't drive her jitters away.

She shook her hands vigorously a few times and opened her mouth wide to release the tension that threatened to clamp down her jaw as tightly as if it were wired. Her heart thumped out the familiar preaudition dance that she called the scared rabbit rhumba. When the stage manager finally beckoned to her, her heart revved up like a record suddenly switched from thirty-three to seventy-eight rpm. The deep breath she took did little good, so she swallowed hard and walked out onto the stage.

"This is Joy Kingsley," the stage manager read from the card. "Her selection is called—" She stopped short and glared at Joy with exasperation. "I'm sorry, ladies and gentlemen," she said to the audience. "There's no title here, just a question mark. Anyway," she continued sarcastically, "Miss Kingsley wrote the 'piece in question' herself."

Joy heard a few unkind sniggers from backstage. *Maybe I shouldn't have tried to bend the rules in my direction*, she thought in a panic. All she'd succeeded in doing since she'd arrived was annoying people. But she was alone on the stage now, and precious seconds were ticking by. *There's no turning back*, she told herself firmly. She strode to center stage, then down to the apron where she sat, dangling her legs over the edge of the stage. She leaned forward to get a closer look at her audience.

The dim houselights cast a pall over the faces of the men and women scattered throughout the orchestra. At best they looked neutral; at worst bleary-eyed and bored. Some of them had taken her picture and résumé from the pile the union had provided at the start of the day and were looking at them desultorily. Others were staring off into space as if they wished they were a million miles away. A few were taking furtive bites from half-eaten sandwiches or sips from containers of what must have been, to judge from the grimace on one woman's face, cold bitter coffee. Not a great house, Joy thought shakily. She quickly scanned the group for a receptive face, but found only one possibility.

It belonged to a man sitting in the fourth row. He had a clipboard balanced on his crossed knee and a pen stuck jauntily behind his right ear. Even at this distance she could tell he was more than usually handsome—wavy sandy-brown hair, eyes a shade lighter, hazel perhaps, straight jaw, strong nose, soft mouth—but what drew her to him was the energy that seemed to radiate from him, in check for the moment but unmistakable and compelling. Though his posture was relaxed, he looked ready to seize—or reject—whatever came his way in an instant. He had been sitting in the theater for a day and a half, just like the others, listening to monologue after monologue, often the same ones over and over again, but he didn't look tired or irritated or anxious for the day to end. Joy's instinct told her that, if she could convince him of her talent and ability, she could convince anyone else in the room as well.

She sought eye contact with him, and although he returned her look readily, she sensed she would have to work hard to retain his attention. "Auditioning an actor with a monologue," she began with more assurance than she felt, "is like judging a painting after seeing only a small corner of it." With a slight raise of his eyebrows, the man conceded the first point and challenged her to continue. "I'm not the corner of a painting," she proclaimed, bringing her hands together and hunching in her shoulders slightly. "I'm an entire canvas, with a full range of colors and shapes, with perspective, meaning and emotion." She brought her arms forward and opened them gracefully, as if to reveal and present her entire self to the audience.

Show me, his eyes said to her. Though he was goading her, she knew she had interested him. It gave her the courage to look away and assess the effect she was having on the rest of the audience. To her surprise and delight, she saw that a few people in the audience had stopped fidgeting or eating or writing or daydreaming. Peering pairs of eyes were focused on her, waiting for her next move. Her nervousness rushed out of her like water through a miner's sieve, leaving golden nuggets of pure energy. "Even if I did a dozen monologues you'd still be seeing only bits and chunks of me, not the whole picture. And I could hardly do a dozen in three minutes. Not," she ad-libbed in a lowered voice, "with a stage manager with a stopwatch—" she looked cautiously over her shoulder "—counting every second."

This garnered some scattered chuckles. Joy looked back at the man and saw him smiling at her, a smile so bright, so dazzling, she actually felt a jolt when she saw it, as if he were returning the energy she was sending into the audience. He nodded, too, as if to say *good work, well done.* It was all the encouragement she needed.

Flying high and free now, Joy jumped up and took complete and confident charge of the stage and her audience. The rest of her piece surged out of her powerfully like electricity from an opened switch. "Some of you may be saying to yourselves, this isn't acting. Who's she trying to kid? I'm not trying to kid anybody, least of all myself. And what I'm doing *is* acting. As an actress I understand and respect the conventions and traditions of the theater."

She then presented evidence in support of her contention. "First, I've created a character—myself, Joy Kingsley." She added as an aside, "I know it doesn't take most playwrights twenty-eight years to create a character, but you have to remember I started from scratch." Her delivery of this line pleased her, and she responded with a laugh as did the audience.

She waited until the laughter had almost died down to continue. "And I've stepped out of the action of the play, my life in this case, like so many characters—from Hamlet to Sheila and Brian in Peter Nichols's *Joe Egg*— to address you, the audience, directly. Most playwrights invent circumstances through which they reveal their characters' actions and emotions. Today, as the playwright, I've chosen to use the actual circumstances of my life."

She paused before moving on to the next beat, or section of the speech. This technique gave her time to shift gears into the next idea and allowed the audience time to assimilate what she had just said. "I don't work nearly enough as an actress. Few of us in this business do. Sure I go to classes and work on scenes with my friends, but I feel like a seed trapped in a vacuum bottle. I'm ready to work, I'm able to work, but I need to plant my feet on a stage." Her voice grew quieter, yet it rang clearly in the near-empty theater, tolling with deeply felt emotion. "I need the soil and rain and air that will allow me to push my way into the world, to grow, to blossom, to die and leave new seeds behind me to a theater alive and strong."

She paused again, let go of her strong emotions and raised her voice to its normal level for the final beat. "My time is nearly up. I haven't given you three minutes of Shakespeare or Ibsen or Clifford Odets. But I have given you myself. I can't offer more than that. And I hope I've shown you in this short time that I have not only talent, verve and originality, but most importantly—the courage of my convictions." She bowed her head to the audience, a gesture of thanks for their attention, turned and strode purposefully offstage.

Not until she reached the wings did her composure crumple. Suddenly she felt weak-kneed and lightheaded with glee. She'd done it! She'd pulled it off! Joy collapsed limply in a folding chair and was soon surrounded by a crowd of actors. "That took guts," one said. "Wish I'd thought of it," another commented. "Tough act to follow," said a third.

A grim-faced fellow walked stiffly past, following the stage manager. "Those who are about to die salute you," he said with mock seriousness. She tipped him a trim military salute.

"Break a leg," she wished him sincerely, and they both broke into a broad grin.

Joy left the theater and strolled slowly down the street. Her triumph might have seemed small to some, but to her it was as tall as the skyscrapers all around her. In those three short minutes on stage she had broken down at least part of the barrier that was keeping her theatrical career from rising above the ground floor. She savored the smack of the winter cold on her cheeks, the crystalline light that poured from the pale sky, the pungent aromas that drifted from the doors of the delicatessens and restaurants she passed. Even the stink of stale beer and smoke that came from the seedier bars on Eighth Avenue didn't seem so bad today.

She couldn't count the times in the past four years that she'd felt she had no control whatsoever over the progress of her career. Casting decisions were frequently made on the basis of hair color or height or whether the producer owed your agent a favor. Like it or not, that's how things worked in show business. It was virtually impossible, especially for a little-known actress like herself, to get around it. But today she had seized a rare opportunity to take matters into her own hands. And she felt great. *Great!* Her step quickened, and soon she was skipping merrily down the street, not exactly sure where she was headed, but in a powerful and joyful hurry to get there.

2

THE SECOND THE LAST AUDITION was over Andy Thornhill shoved his papers and notebook into his briefcase and bolted. Two days of doing the same thing hour after hour, cooped up in the same place, was too much. Next year he'd send someone else to cover the auditions and stay back at the Arc where he belonged. He ducked out the stage door and up the alley and lost himself in the rush hour crowd, glad that he'd managed to avoid the inevitable invitations for drinks or dinner from his colleagues. All he wanted was a couple of cold beers and a meal before he drove back to Philadelphia. He'd been away from the theater for only forty-eight hours, but that was forty-eight hours too long.

Andy headed straight for K.C.'s, where he liked the feel of sawdust under his feet. It was real and substantial, unlike so much in New York. He strode straight through to the dining room and ordered a beer from a passing waiter even before settling himself at a table near the wall. Service was quick in the almost empty room, and he downed half the icy brew in a single gulp. When he put the glass down, his mouth, even his teeth, felt deliciously cold, almost numb, and his mind had begun to recover from the dulling sameness of the past two days.

The time hadn't been entirely wasted, though, he thought as he munched a couple of peanuts from the wooden bowl on the table. He'd almost certainly found the actress he needed for Gerry Westover's new play. Joy Kingsley. He wouldn't forget that name in a hurry. She'd caught his attention the minute she'd strode onto the stage. He liked the way she walked, the way she looked, those long, long legs, that flowing chestnut mane. She reminded him of a fine thoroughbred filly. All she needed was to be given her head and she'd fly away with the part like the wind.

He glanced at his watch. If she could meet him here in half an hour, they could eat and talk about working at the Arc. Talent and suitability for a role were only part of what he looked for; attitude, dedication and spirit were important, too. He usually waited until a few days after the audition to talk to an actor, but time was short now with rehearsals scheduled to start next week. Anyway, his instinct told him Joy Kingsley was everything he was looking for. And more. He couldn't deny that she interested him as much as a woman as an actress. She'd been on his mind all afternoon. But he moved those feelings to the back burner. The important thing now was casting the part and getting back to the theater. He ordered another beer and headed into the bar to use the pay phone.

WHEN THE PHONE RANG, Joy danced out of the kitchen and across the room. "If this is the restaurant," she sang to the tune of the Stephen Sondheim song that was playing on the stereo, "they can forget it if they want me to come in for someone else tonight." She waved the wire whisk she'd been using to make a salad dressing in time to the music. "Hello," she chimed into the phone.

"You sound like you're in a good mood," said a male voice she didn't recognize.

"The best," she answered gaily. The unfamiliar voice had a slight rasp to it, not at all unpleasant, but rather sexy, like the feel of a man's face before he's shaved in the morning. "Who is this?" she asked. She couldn't match a face—shaved or unshaved—to the voice.

"Andy Thornhill."

She recognized the name immediately. Anyone who took the theater seriously knew the reputation he'd built for his Arc Theater. She'd give her entire collection of original cast albums for a chance to work there. He must have been at the auditions that afternoon. She cradled the receiver between her chin and one hunched shoulder and crossed the fingers of both hands. "What can I do for you?" she asked coolly.

"Well," he said with a short laugh, "since you put it that way, have dinner with me."

Deflated and disappointed, Joy said coldly, "I see."

Andy heaved a long-suffering sigh. It annoyed him that New York actresses were so wary, but then again he couldn't really blame them. And given some of the thoughts he'd been having about this one, she had every right to be cool, he told himself wryly. "I can hear what you're thinking all the way over here. But I'll tell you right off the bat, I'm not that kind of guy. I've got a script to show you. I'm also starving and I need to get back to Philadelphia tonight. Can you be at K.C.'s in half an hour?"

Joy wasn't used to having her mind read over the telephone, but script was the magic word. She forced the eagerness out of her voice. "Do you always do two things at once?" she asked casually.

"Whenever possible," he answered impatiently. "Does that mean you'll be there?"

"How will I know you when I get there?"

"You'll recognize me," he said with another staccato laugh. "I'm the one you used to get started this afternoon."

Joy was still reeling from his last remark when she realized he'd hung up. So the sandy-haired hunk was Andy Thornhill. She'd been wondering who he was all afternoon, musing on those expressive hazel eyes, the energy he exuded from every pore. She couldn't have picked a better target this afternoon if she'd tried. Andy Thornhill. She rolled the name around in her mouth. It definitely had a ring to it.

She had gone back into the kitchen when the momentousness of the phone call stopped her in her tracks. What was she doing? She had to get dressed and get to K.C.'s. To talk to Andy Thornhill about a script. *A script!* She tore off a length of plastic wrap and fitted it over her salad, dumped the dressing into a plastic container and hurried to her closet.

Twenty minutes later she was dressed in a green-gray gaucho-style skirt, a flowing cream-colored over-blouse cinched at the waist with a wide leather belt, and handsome leather riding boots. Against the cold night air she armed herself with an enormous woolen shawl and a brown slouch hat.

She bounced down Ninth Avenue to Restaurant Row—Forty-sixth Street between Ninth and Tenth Avenues—where K.C.'s was just one of many restaurants located on the ground floor of the block's restored brownstones, and paused before the well-worn wooden door that was all too familiar to her. Before going off to do summer stock in New Hampshire the previous summer, she had waited tables here. But maybe, just maybe, her waitressing days were over. Jauntily she swung the door open and stepped inside.

The first thing to hit her was the smell of grilling meat, which she inhaled as deeply and with as much pleasure as a fine perfume. As she passed the bar, the bartender, another "at liberty" actor, greeted her by name. "Looking for a job?" he kidded. Returning from New Hampshire last September, Joy had been disappointed to find there were no openings.

"Yeah," Joy said with a smile. "But not here, Charlie." She moved toward him and lowered her voice. "I'm meeting Andy Thornhill."

Charlie let out a long, low whistle. "Nice going. How'd you swing that?"

"Had an audition today."

"Through your agent?"

"What agent? You mean that guy who never returns my phone calls? No, the Equity regional theater auditions."

At the opposite end of the bar two waitresses were calling for Charlie to fill the orders for their tables. "Gotta go, Joy. My public clamors," he said with a dramatic gesture.

Joy passed through the bar into the dining room at the rear, enjoying the crunch of the sawdust under the soles of her boots. She'd hated the stuff when she'd worked here, but tonight it felt like a plush red carpet. The back room was as spare and simple as ever—whitewashed brick walls thick with theater posters, round tables covered with red checkered cloths and old-fashioned saloon-style chairs. The room was only half full now, but later, when the theaters let out, there would hardly be room for the staff to pass among the tables.

She spotted Andy Thornhill at a table by the far wall, seated under a poster for the Dustin Hoffman revival of *Death of a Salesman*. The moment she saw him she experienced a jolt much like the one she'd felt that afternoon on the stage, as if he had given her an instant energy transfusion merely by being present in a room. He was too involved in whatever he was writing in a large black notebook to notice that she'd arrived, and she took a few seconds to compose herself. Even across the room he gave off an air of intensity that made her breathe deeper and harder. Feeling warm and flushed and not altogether comfortable, she removed her shawl and hat and left them on the rack by the entrance to the dining room. Having seen him again, she realized her excitement wasn't entirely due to the prospect of a job. There was something about the man himself that was just as compelling.

Andy looked up from the notes he was jotting to see her standing across the room. As she approached him, he experienced a curious elation, as if he had just learned that a drawing he'd bought simply because it had appealed to him had turned out to be an original Matisse, a priceless treasure. In that outfit she looked like the heroine of a historical novel set in colonial Mexico. He invoked his director's prerogative and cast himself as the hero who would carry her into the golden sunset.

Joy felt his eyes on her as she crossed the room. His scrutiny made her as self-conscious as she had been the first time she'd worked in front of a camera, aware that no detail of anything she wore or said or did would be missed. When she reached the table, he rose and extended his hand. "Glad you could make it," he said huskily. "Very glad."

"My pleasure," she said softly. His fingers closed strongly around hers and his eyes beckoned her nearer. Resisting his silent invitation was like keeping two magnets apart. She managed, though the attraction was strong.

Close up he was even more handsome than he'd been at a distance. His eyes were laced with flecks of gold that shimmered and danced like sunlight on a pond. She studied them for several seconds until her hand began to tingle. She was breathless, too, and light-headed. The sensations were not entirely welcome, and she snatched her hand away. Like every serious young actress, she had to be all too careful of the casting couch. Its cushions were always stuffed with unpleasant, uncomfortable, unhealthy material. She sat on the chair he held out for her, but edged it away from him warily.

So she felt it, too, he thought when he saw her move the chair. Her sudden skittishness annoyed him. So what if some sparks had flown between them? They could still conduct themselves like professionals. "I won't bite," he assured her tartly.

"I didn't think you would," she retorted.

"Sure you did, or you wouldn't have moved your chair. Like I told you on the phone, I don't take advantage of actresses. I don't have the time."

"Meaning that if you had the time you would?"

Andy Thornhill leaned back in his chair. "Your point," he conceded with a laugh. He tipped the chair back on its rear legs and gave a self-deprecating chuckle. *Don't get this dinner off on the wrong foot*, he admonished himself. *Whatever you're feeling isn't as important as casting Gerry's play.*

"I guess I didn't expect you to act like you just got off the bus from Peoria," he said honestly. "Not after that audition this afternoon. Unlike most people in this business, I don't hand out empty compliments like penny candy, but I've got to say that was one helluva performance."

"Thank you," Joy said shortly. She was still put out by his earlier behavior and was tempted, instead of enjoying the compliment, to make a caustic remark about not knowing where he'd found the time to make it. But she knew it was her nervousness about the meeting—and about the unwanted sensations that lingered in her body—that would be talking, so she held her tongue.

Andy signaled to their waiter and ordered another beer for himself and the glass of red wine Joy requested. "So where *did* you get off the bus from?" he asked casually, as if they'd never had their little run-in.

His quick and total change in attitude amazed her. The man clearly wasted no time on leftover emotions; when something was finished he forgot it and moved on. Joy had often wished she were more like that, but emotions stayed with her. Like food, they had to be tasted, swallowed, digested, used up. But she tried to match his easy tone as she answered, "Central Connecticut. I got my Equity card as a teenage apprentice at the local summer theater. After I graduated from Northwestern, I came to New York."

"How long have you been here?"

"Four years this September."

"And how's it going?"

"You saw my résumé. Not as well as I'd like," she said frankly.

"Why is that?" he probed.

"You sure get right to the point," she hedged. She had never met anyone so disarmingly honest, who said exactly what he thought and asked for exactly what he wanted. His manner wasn't demanding or aggressive, because he seemed genuinely interested in the answers to his questions. But still Joy felt the need to hang back, as if she were on the threshold of an enticing room she wasn't sure she wanted to enter.

Andy sipped the beer the waiter had just served and munched a few more nuts, waiting for her answer, but willing to let her get to it in her own time.

Joy drank some of her wine. Any of the pat answers she could give—tough competition, too many actors for too few jobs, a lousy agent—would be an insult to Andy Thornhill's intelligence and his interest in her. But she couldn't refuse to answer his question, even if it meant revealing more of herself than felt comfortable at the moment. "I really don't know," she said finally. "It's not that I don't work at all. I've had some good jobs, but not enough of them, and they don't seem to get me very far." As she spoke he looked at her intently, and the light in his eyes grew, the way sunlight enters a room as a shade is gradually raised. "It's as if—" she paused to think of a vivid way to express how she felt "—I can get my motor started and go chugging down the road, but when I get a certain distance it stalls. And I don't know what the trouble is. Maybe what I need," she finished dryly, "is a good mechanic."

They both laughed, and Joy saw a flash of admiration and excitement in Andy Thornhill's eyes that made her glad she had spoken openly. Something was happening to her, something fragile and elusive she couldn't find a name for. Their laughter died down quickly, but the look that followed on its heels stretched on and on.

"I'm getting very hungry," Andy said quietly, not taking his eyes from her. For the first time since she'd sat at the table, Joy had the feeling he was not saying exactly what he meant. She shifted her gaze. "Shall we order?" he suggested.

"Sure," she mumbled, and glued her eyes to the blackboard on the wall where the day's menu was written.

When the waiter had left their table, Andy said matter-of-factly, "I think you need a good road map."

It took Joy a second to realize what he was talking about. She was still coasting downhill on the look they had exchanged, but he'd already shifted gears and was talking about her career again.

"A change of direction," he continued. "Or rather, a clear direction. You've been hopping all over the place." From memory he ran down the jobs listed on her résumé. "There's no continuity. You take anything that comes along."

"Of course I do," Joy countered. "I have to. I don't get that many opportunities to work."

"Opportunities," he said emphatically, "are where you make them."

"That's easy for you to say," Joy charged. "You're running the show. I've got to find a show before I can work."

"And the only way you're going to do that is by taking risks—like you did today." Suddenly his look changed from serious to spritely. "Watching you," he said with a grin, "was like being let out of a musty old closet. You were refreshing and free and—" he paused to choose the right word "—intriguing." His look changed yet again, from spritely to searching, and Joy felt herself begin to glow.

"Intriguing?" she questioned. "I wasn't trying to be mysterious. Quite the opposite, in fact."

"I feel the same way now. That you keep part of yourself in reserve. You don't have to hide anything from me, Joy."

"You don't make it easy to," she said when she recovered the breath he had taken away. "Maybe that's why I'm trying so hard," she added, speaking as much to herself as to him.

They both fell silent as the waiter slid a steaming bowl of pasta in front of Joy and a steak in front of Andy. Immediately he picked up his fork and knife and began to eat, as absorbed in his food as he had been in her only a moment before. Joy took a few small bites of her pasta and considered the man sitting beside her, trying to imagine what it would be like to work for someone so intent and single-minded. Difficult, she decided, but exhilarating, like skiing a tricky and unknown trail. And what would it be like to have an affair with him? The looks they had exchanged could clearly take them in that direction, only the danger there would lie in a broken heart, not broken limbs. However, an affair was clearly and utterly out of the question. Taking a sideways glance at him, though— the strong line of his jaw, the laugh lines etched lightly around his eyes, the clear glow in his hazel eyes—Joy knew why the thought had come to her. The same thought would have occurred to any healthy, red-blooded female confronted with so fine a specimen of the human male.

"I caught the new Marsha Norman play last night," Andy remarked. "Have you seen it?"

"On opening night. I have a friend in the cast," Joy explained. "What did you think of it?"

"I was going to ask you the same thing," he replied.

"I asked you first," Joy returned, smiling.

"So you did."

They talked about the play for a long time and about other plays written by the same author, who had started her career at a regional theater in St. Louis. Andy held that the true impulse for innovation in the American theater was at regional theaters like his. Joy maintained that sooner or later, in order to join the mainstream, every theater professional ended up in the hub—New York. They argued the point back and forth, bringing their brains, emotions and personal experiences to bear on the freewheeling discussion. Joy felt stretched and tested in a way she hadn't been for far too long. She was using all her resources—intelligence, quick thinking, logic, knowledge—to match Andy's considerable skills. And she was more than holding her own against a tough opponent.

They might have continued the discussion for hours longer, but the decibel level in the restaurant had risen precipitously, and she was shouting to be heard. "Where did all these people come from? The theaters can't be out already."

Andy looked at his watch. "Hell's bells," he swore. "I'm supposed to be in Philadelphia now. To meet with my set designer."

"At ten-thirty?" Joy asked incredulously.

"I've been gone for two days," he said. "We're on a very tight schedule."

"Do you always work this late?"

"This is early," he declared, not entirely joking.

"And what do you do for fun?"

His expression softened. "Have dinner with lovely, lively, intelligent actresses," he said quietly, reaching out to draw his finger lightly along her cheek. Joy shivered, as if a chilly wave had swept over her and the next one might carry her out to an even colder sea. Andy looked down at his hand and drew it away quickly, as if her face had suddenly become hot. He signaled vigorously for the waiter. "We still haven't talked about this script," he said, all business again. "Let's go someplace quiet and I'll tell you about it." He tossed a credit card to the waiter and said to Joy as he left the table, "Be right back. Have to make a phone call."

"I COULD USE a cup of coffee if it isn't any trouble," Andy said as Joy snapped shut the locks on her apartment door. She wasn't entirely happy about bringing him there, but it was the only really quiet place she could think of in the neighborhood.

"No trouble at all." She hung their coats on the oak rack beside the door and hurried into the kitchen to put the water on.

"Nice place," Andy remarked, making himself comfortable on the love seat. "Homey. Hard to believe we're in a modern high rise. Except for the view of course."

With her limited resources, Joy had worked hard to give her room an air of old-fashioned comfort and charm. For convenience and efficiency many people in studio apartments used sofa beds or built loft beds, but Joy had bought an old iron bedstead in a thrift shop, painted it white and covered it with a bright patchwork quilt. To separate the bed from the rest of her room, she'd found a mahogany-framed translucent screen. A soft, delicious light passed through it in the morning when she awakened. There was also a rolltop desk, its cubbyholes stuffed with letters and postcards and stationery, and beside it a golden oak bookcase, its glass-covered shelves packed tight with books and scripts.

The love seat where Andy Thornhill sat was covered with flowered chintz slipcovers she'd made herself from fabric unearthed in the back room of a postage stamp of a shop on the Lower East Side. The occasional tables and coffee table that flanked it—all rescued from the street and refinished by Joy—were covered with vases of dried flowers, half-read books and magazines and the whimsical trinkets and toys Joy loved to collect. The walls were hung with a mélange of old theatrical posters and prints and faded photographs.

"Thanks," Joy called from the kitchen. "My mother calls it early thrift shop."

Andy's laugh rippled through the room. "I take it she doesn't approve. And not just of your interior decorating."

"It's more that she worries," she replied, impressed by his perceptiveness. "You know the scenario—youngest daughter alone in the big city, without a proper job, and 'no prospects'—as she so delicately puts it."

"Meaning no husband," Andy said bluntly.

Joy let the comment pass. "Milk and sugar?" she asked.

"Black," he answered. But he wasn't going to let the subject drop. "My mother's the same way. Keeps wondering when I'm going to 'settle down.'"

Joy laughed and brought the coffee tray into the main room. "Do you think our mothers know each other?"

"No, they just belong to the Universal Mothers' Club, Weird Children Chapter."

Joy laughed again and moved a few things on the coffee table to make room for the tray. "Were you the family weirdo, too?" She sat beside him and handed him his mug.

"Still am." He blew a couple of cooling breaths on the hot coffee and took a sip. "No, that's unfair. In the last few years, since I've started to gain a reputation in the business, the family's come around. But I'm the only unmarried, childless son, and my mother's worried I'll end up as some sort of theatrical monk." He let out a short laugh. He was feeling decidedly unmonklike at the moment. If they didn't get started on that script soon, he might well find himself making the love seat they were sitting on live up to its name.

"What's so funny?" Joy asked, thinking to herself that it would be hard for any woman—mother or no—to worry about Andy Thornhill becoming a monk. It would take a tremendous effort to sublimate the sexual energy she was all too aware of at the moment.

"Just imagining myself in a cowl," he said, reaching for his briefcase. "Pretty incongruous picture," he muttered as he pulled out a copy of the script.

Joy restrained herself from agreeing as she took the script from him. Just feeling the weight of it in her hand released a surge of excitement in her, and she ran her index finger over the embossed letters of the title. She started to fold back the maroon cover, but Andy stopped her.

"We'll get to the script in a minute. What I really want to talk to you about is the Arc itself. I'm looking for a commitment to ensemble work as much as talent. I don't have time for prima donnas, Joy. If all you want from the Arc is a good credit on your résumé, I don't want you. The work we do together as a company is the

most important thing to me. I'm not trying to get anywhere. I'm trying to create a working theater. If that's
not what you want, don't waste my time, don't waste
your own time."

"I'm not in the habit of wasting my time," she said
stiffly. There was no need to lecture as if she were a
schoolgirl.

"Don't be offended. I say this to everyone I audition—even people like you, who probably don't need
to hear it. It prevents misunderstandings. I like to put
my cards on the table."

And hold the deck, too, she thought. But perhaps she
was being too touchy. There were plenty of actors, talented actors, who did take jobs more for their value as
stepping-stones than the work itself. "I understand,"
she relented.

"Good," he said. Then he began to talk about the
play, a drama about two half sisters, one much older
than the other, who meet again after a long separa-
tion. "Each of them has her own myth about the man
who was their father, and both hold on to it tena-
ciously—" he made two tight fists to illustrate his point
"—until the action of the play forces them to admit to
the truth." He relaxed his hand but not his focus as he
continued to speak about the sisters' relationship with
each other, with their respective husbands, with their
parents, who appear in flashbacks, and how they are
changed by the events of the play.

He was totally involved in what he was saying, and
Joy entered the world he described easily. As she listened and watched him—for he spoke as eloquently
with his body as his voice—she made notes to herself,
filing away information that would be useful in the
preparation of her audition scenes.

"The script I'm giving you is far from a finished product. Gerry will be working with us during the rehearsal process, so of course I'm looking for someone who can help create a character, not just interpret the playwright's finished product. I've cast all the parts already, except the younger sister, Barbara. And I've worked with everyone in the cast before, so how you fit in will also be a consideration. Why don't you prepare the last scene in act one and the second scene in act two?" he suggested as he reached again for his briefcase and took out a black leather appointment book. "How's Friday at three?"

Joy didn't have to check her book to know it was fine. Even if she had another appointment she'd have broken it—except perhaps an audition for a Broadway show. "I think I can just about squeeze you in," she said dryly.

He grinned at her. "You don't have to play hard to get with me, Joy."

"That's a relief," she shot back. They both laughed, and another charged glance passed between them.

Andy stood suddenly. He was overtired and far too susceptible to the feelings he was starting to have about her. "I'd better be going. It's a long drive and it's been a hectic couple of days."

Joy followed him to the door and handed him his scarf and jacket from the rack. "Drive carefully," she said, feeling more protective than she knew she ought to. "And thanks for dinner."

"Thanks for joining me," he said softly. The urge to kiss her good-night was getting stronger by the second. He stifled it but not the urge to push a stray wisp of hair off her right cheek. Her eyes wavered as his fingers lingered on her warm skin, but he was the one to finally break the connection. "Take care," he said, and left quickly.

Joy closed the door quietly behind him, leaning on it for a moment until her pounding heart slowed. She knew she ought to be tired, but despite the late hour and her lack of sleep the previous night she was too keyed up from the day's events to even think of going to bed. And lying there trying to fall asleep would only give her vivid and powerful imagination a chance to start spinning fantasies about Andy Thornhill.

She changed into a cozy flannel nightgown—fashioned to warm the body and produce cool, modest thoughts—and took a pad and pencil from her desk. She curled up on the love seat, opened the script and began to read. After the first scene she knew that Andy Thornhill had given her the opportunity to audition for the role of a lifetime. She read on eagerly, jotting page after page of notes on character, physical and emotional circumstances, background, ideas flowing like water after the spring thaw.

Three hours later she stretched her cramped legs and walked stiffly to the window. Her back ached and her fingers were numb from writing, but her mind was charged with energy and resolve. She was going to do everything she could to get this part, and she wasn't going to let her attraction to Andy Thornhill get in the way. Attractions came and went, life was full of them, but roles that fit like fine kid gloves were a rare find.

DRIVING DOWN the New Jersey Turnpike, Andy wished there was some way he could put the car on automatic pilot. All he'd done since getting in the car was think about Joy. If the car could drive itself, he could read or write, immerse himself in some other task. He'd tried to think about any number of the hundred things he needed to think about, wanted to think about, but they all bowed to Joy, the queen of his thoughts tonight.

It had been a long time since he'd felt so strong a pull toward a woman. Not that he lived the monklike existence his mother feared. Far from it. But the Arc was his first priority, his first love.

Only one woman had ever challenged that. Challenged but lost, although she hadn't been the only loser in that match. No, Brenda had been the winner, he the loser. If they had married she'd have been miserable. He had loved her so much and had had such a strong vision of their future together that he'd set about creating it the same way he had created the Arc, never even considering the possibility that her vision had been different from his. He had been so single-minded in his desire to build the future that he had disregarded the present. When she left him he was shocked.

He thought back to the way it had started with Brenda. His attraction to her had been sparked as quickly as today's attraction to Joy. He hoped, he prayed that whatever happened between them, if anything were to happen between them, he would be able to let the relationship evolve naturally and not try to direct it as if it were a play. He was too impatient with life, too tempted to shape it into neat segments that resembled scenes and acts in a never-ending drama.

Don't give in to the temptation, he warned himself. *You can't mold people the way you mold characters.* If anything developed between himself and Joy, it would have to be right for both of them. He thought again of her crossing the room in K.C.'s tonight and of riding off into the sunset with her, her arms clasped around his waist, her chestnut hair flying in the wind. He laughed at his romantic notion and reminded himself that no matter how dashing a hero he was, getting her onto the back of his horse wouldn't mean anything if she didn't want to be there.

3

FROM THE STREET the theater looked deserted, the only sign of life the red-and-white Arc banner that fluttered in the wind high over Joy's head. She walked up the gray stone steps to a pair of arched doorways, painted the same red as the banner, and tried one of the handles, a large circle of iron, chillingly cold against her ungloved hand. Her teeth chattered involuntarily, and she gave the handle a hard twist to the right and pushed against the door with her shoulder. It was not only open but gave easily, and she was propelled awkwardly into the theater lobby. The door clattered shut behind her.

"Can I help you?"

The disembodied voice seemed to be coming from the rafters of the dim cavernous room. For a moment Joy had a spooky feeling until her eyes adjusted and she noticed a light in the box office window on the far left of the lobby. She let out a nervous little laugh and started toward the window. "Hi, I didn't see you at first. I'm Joy Kingsley. I have an audition at three. Am I in the right place?" She peered in through the window and saw a young woman in jeans and a plaid flannel shirt sorting tickets at a battered gray metal desk.

"You sure are. Andy's in the theater reading someone now. Pull up a pew," she invited with a friendly smile. "He'll be with you soon. I don't think he's running too late."

Joy thanked her and dropped her large purse on the nearest plain mahogany pew, presumably salvaged when Andy had first turned the abandoned church into a theater. She started to take off her coat, but the lobby was chilly, and now that she'd heard there were others auditioning for the part, she was battling her own preaudition shivers, so she wrapped the coat closer around her and hugged her arms to her chest. She didn't know why she had assumed she would be the only person reading for the part that afternoon. Andy had never said she would be. Wishful thinking, that was it.

She paced the lobby, stopping to look at the pictures that lined the wall separating the lobby from the theater. It was like reading a history of the Arc, from its struggling shoestring days to the comparative wealth it now enjoyed as one of the country's premier regional theaters. But even with more money to spend on sets and costumes and lighting, it was clear that the Arc's director did not strive first for theatrical effect. The productions were clean and spare, putting the play and players front and center.

She was thinking how proud she would be to have her picture on this wall when the door to the right side of the theater opened. A woman who was very much her "type"—brunette, attractive, intelligent-looking— walked out. She stopped when she reached the lobby to pull a knit cap out of her purse and noticed Joy. The two exchanged a frankly appraising look, sizing up the competition. The other woman gave her a patronizing smile and slowly put on her cap and gloves.

The gesture was calculated to make Joy nervous, but she had learned not to let other actors intimidate her before an audition. She slipped out of her coat and sat nonchalantly on the pew where she'd left her purse.

When the other woman saw Joy ignoring her, she turned up her coat collar and left. The episode had served, though, to indicate how soon she would be entering the theater. She took her script from her bag and laid it on her lap. Closing her eyes, she silently reviewed the scenes she had prepared, letting her imagination transport her into the circumstances of the play.

Suddenly a door from the theater swung open. Joy heard the noise and returned abruptly to reality. Her eyes flew open, and she saw Andy Thornhill stride through the door. "Hello!" she said, unexpectedly breathless at the sight of him.

She was lovelier than he'd remembered, though the image of her hadn't strayed far from his mind these past couple of days. Her color was heightened to a delicate rose by the cold—and probably by a case of preaudition nerves as well. "Hi," he said, deliberately greeting her with less warmth than he felt. It was going to be hard to live up to the promise he'd made to take things slowly with her. "Make yourself comfortable. I'll be back in a few minutes."

Joy leaned back against the pew, deflated. He hadn't even seemed to know who she was. He'd probably been seeing actresses all day, and one looked more or less like another by now. She realized she'd been far too confident about getting this job. Just because the director had taken her to dinner—and had seemed somewhat taken with her—didn't mean he was going to hand her the role on a silver platter. She'd have to earn it.

Ten long minutes passed, which she tried to fill by reviewing the scenes she was going to read. But she was beset by a full-fledged case of the jitters that made concentration difficult. Finally the outside door opened, and Andy came back into the lobby.

"Sorry to keep you waiting," he said. His smile was cordial but only distantly related to the looks he had beamed at her two nights ago. "Will you come into the theater now?" He waited for her to rise and precede him to the door, which he politely opened for her.

Joy marched numbly down the aisle of the theater. She had let her expectations for this audition—and of Andy Thornhill—get far too high and now she was paying the price. She realized how much the turn of events had affected her when Andy called out to introduce her to someone whose presence she hadn't even noticed.

"This is Gretchen Weiler, our stage manager. Gretchen, this is Joy Kingsley."

Gretchen, slim and boyish, with short-cropped curly blond hair, rose energetically from her aisle seat in the third row and thrust an unadorned hand at Joy, surprising her with the strength of her grip.

"Gretchen will be reading with you this afternoon, Joy. If you're ready, I'd like to get started."

"Of course," Joy said, hoping her voice didn't sound as raspy as it felt in her throat. She put her coat and purse on the nearest seat and gripped her script tightly.

Gretchen, in sneakers and jeans, stepped onto the stage with a single nimble bound. Joy had dressed as she thought her character—a small-town schoolteacher— would in a plain skirt and sweater and low heels. She smoothed her skirt, adjusted the sleeves of her sweater and began the audition. As the sedate seemingly implacable Barbara, she mounted a small flight of steps at the front of the stage and took her place in the glare of the single bare light bulb.

"We'll start on page fifteen with Madeline's entrance," Andy directed.

Joy could hear his voice coming from somewhere in the front of the house but couldn't see him in the darkness. She took a deep silent breath and waited for Gretchen to feed her the first line. The stage manager gave her the cue in a clear, uninflected voice; she was there to read the lines, not to act, but Joy had to respond to her in the same way she would respond to another actor. Not only did she have to imagine that this bare stage was the living room of the house Barbara had lived in all her life, but she also had to endow Gretchen with all the characteristics of her much older, little known half sister. In the scene the sisters reveal that they each believe in entirely different versions of the same event. With increasing emotion, Madeline tries to convince Barbara of the truth of her version, but Barbara refuses to be moved.

Joy had chosen to use an image technique in this scene, playing Barbara as if she were a rock on the shore. No matter how much the waves—Madeline— crashed over her she would hold her ground. The waves might erode her, change her shape somewhat, but they would not get her to roll over and reveal her underside.

She and Gretchen got through two pages of the scene when Andy interrupted her in midsentence. She looked out into the darkness and discerned a shadowy figure at the center front of the house. "I see what you're trying to do here, Joy, but it's too static. Do you have a scarf or a handkerchief or something?"

"In my purse," she answered. Inside, her stomach was sinking. He wouldn't hire her if he thought she made boring choices. But she reminded herself that every audition was different. Some directors just wanted you to read the scene. Others wanted to see how you took direction, how adaptable you were. Well, if he wanted adaptable, she'd give him adaptable. "I'll get it."

"You've heard the phrase 'blind panic'?" he asked as she stepped into the audience to get her scarf. "That's what Barbara is in. Give the scarf to Gretchen and turn your back to the house," he instructed when she got back to the stage.

The next thing she knew, Gretchen had covered Joy's eyes and was moving her around the stage until she had lost all sense of orientation. She felt Gretchen back away from her, and a sense of panic did begin to overtake her. There was absolute silence in the theater; she had no idea which way she was facing, where Gretchen and Andy were. She put her hands out in front of her and began to grope uncertainly at the air around her. When she found no obstacles in any direction, she took a tentative step forward, testing the ground with her foot. If she was close to the edge of the stage, she might fall off. Although she knew it wasn't far to tumble, with her eyes covered her sense of distance and depth was obscured and she felt fearful.

From a far corner of the stage she heard Gretchen deliver the first line of the scene. Although she hadn't memorized the lines, she knew the gist of them. She turned toward the sound of Gretchen's voice and answered her. The next cue came from another direction. Andy must have instructed the stage manager to keep moving. Joy pivoted again and answered with an approximate version of Barbara's response. The next line was a long time coming; Joy found herself wondering where it would come from, or after a while even if it would come. When Gretchen's voice rang out from behind and above her, her first impulse was to wheel around and meet it, but a stronger instinct told her to stay where she was. *Aha,* she said to herself. *That's what he was driving at. My choice wasn't bad, but I didn't go far enough. Barbara may hold her ground, but it's because she's fighting a blind panic.*

She delivered her response and stayed still. Gretchen's next cue came quickly, still behind her, but now to the left. Deliberately Joy aimed her words in the opposite direction, fending off the waves she felt, but not impervious to them as she had been in her first reading.

"Okay, stop," Andy called. "Take off the scarf, Joy. Give her a script, Gretchen, and start the scene again."

This time Joy played the scene using the emotional underpinnings she had learned from the exercise. She had a clear sense of what she was trying to accomplish and she acted from that. A chilling amount of tension built up during the scene, and she stepped away from Gretchen with an almost palpable relief when it was over.

She expected some feedback from Andy when they had finished, but all she heard from the house was a long silence and then, "Next scene, please."

Joy's well-thumbed script fell open to the other scene she had studied, the climax of the play where Barbara and Madeline finally acknowledge that their father was neither of the mythical figures they had believed in but a more or less ordinary man.

She started reading the scene with the caution required of crossing a mine field, stepping carefully from line to line, feeling her way. As she was about to turn to the second page of the scene, Andy appeared at the bottom of the stage.

"Stop, Joy, what are you scared of?" he demanded.

"The scene's a mine field," she said, defending her choice firmly.

"Right! Good image! But you're never going to get to the other side the way you're doing it."

"The point is not just to get to the other side, but to get there alive, in one piece," she maintained.

"Forget getting killed, forget getting hurt, forget about everything but getting there. Find the courage and do it. Now start again," he commanded.

He retreated into the darkness, and Joy tamped down her annoyance. He was bullying her like a tough drill sergeant with a raw recruit. She didn't like it, but she pushed her personal feelings away and put her attention on the scene. She did a brief image exercise in her mind, picturing herself in jungle fatigues at the edge of a mine field. She fixed the safety point in the distance and imagined herself crossing the field and getting there. Then she cleared her mind again and began to read.

Once more Andy's idea and direction energized the solid foundation of her own preparatory work. By focusing on the completion of a strong action, the emotional highs and lows of the scene emerged with more clarity and sharpness than she had attained in her own rehearsals. When she reached the end of the scene, she was tired, drained, but knew she had turned in some very good work. Her only reward, however, was a "Thank you, Joy," in the dismissive tone she had heard far too many times to mistake its meaning.

She walked slowly off the stage, picked up her coat and purse and started up the aisle. Even if she hadn't gotten the job, she told herself stoutly, she'd given a terrific audition, and that was no small accomplishment.

"Can you wait in the lobby for a few minutes, please?" Andy asked offhandedly as she passed the row where he was sitting. He hardly looked up from the notes he was scribbling on a yellow legal pad.

Joy nodded and proceeded up the aisle. He probably wanted to let her down easily, tell her all the reasons why he would like to hire her but couldn't. There were always a million reasons, and they were always more or less arbitrary. She went into the lobby and plumped down on a cold hard pew. She didn't want him to be nice to her, she wanted him to hire her; she didn't want apologies, she wanted a job. And she didn't want to hear why she couldn't have it. She didn't want his explanations to diminish her knowledge that she had done the best job she could have done today. She would leave before she had to listen to any painfully feeble excuses. She stood and stuffed her arms into the sleeves of her coat, slammed her hat down on her head and hefted her purse.

She had started toward the door when the theater door flew open and Andy stepped into the lobby, script and yellow pad under his left arm, pen stuck behind his right ear. "Rehearsals start Monday morning at ten. The pay is the union minimum and I don't negotiate on that. But you get a free room, which most theaters don't offer."

Joy's feet felt as if they were cemented to the floor. She couldn't move until she was sure she'd heard correctly. "Does this mean I have the part?"

"You're going to have to do something to earn the munificent salary I just offered you," he returned with a grin.

"Really?" she asked, her voice rising to a pitch just short of a squeal of delight.

"Really," he reiterated.

"Oh! Oh, dear," she spluttered, moved to simultaneous laughter and tears of joy. "Thank you. Thank you so much."

"No, it's I who should thank you. You're going to be a splendid Barbara." He took a few steps toward her. "Welcome to the Arc, Joy." He started to extend his right hand to hers, but the gesture grew and he took both her hands in both of his.

"I'm so glad to be here," she said solemnly, her glistening eyes meeting his. They looked deeply, searchingly at each other, moving imperceptibly closer with each passing second, as if some inexorable force were pulling them together.

"Andy? Are you there?" Gretchen's curly head popped through the door to the theater.

The force pulling them together disappeared as quickly as it had arisen, and Andy dropped Joy's hands. Joy thought she saw a brief shadow pass over Gretchen's face. Her hands were suddenly cold and clammy, and she shoved them deep into the pockets of her coat.

"What is it?" Andy asked.

"Do you want to see what Larry's fixed up in the shop? He had to redesign the door. It works a little differently now, and he wants you to see it before he installs it. The cast will probably need to work with it before the performance tonight."

"I'll be down in a minute," he told Gretchen. When the door closed, he turned back to Joy and explained. "We were having some problems with the set for the current production. It's a wonderful new romantic farce called *Bananas Over You.*"

She chuckled appreciatively at the title. "It sounds like a latter-day Marx Brothers' vehicle."

"With a soupçon of Noël Coward thrown in for good measure. Want to come along with me?" he invited. "See where you'll be spending the next couple of months?" He didn't want her to leave so very soon, even knowing she'd be back in a few days.

"Sure," Joy said with alacrity, and passed through the door he held open for her.

"I've tried to keep as much of the flavor of the old church as I could," he told her. "After all, the theater has its origins in religion, and it's always good to stay in touch with your roots." He pointed up at the untouched arched and vaulted ceiling that remained an inspiring canopy for audience and actors. "Up until two years ago we used the original pews for seating, but then we got a grant for improvement of the physical plant and put in these new plush seats." They were well-padded and covered with a tightly woven cardinal-red fabric.

"You sound almost disappointed," Joy remarked.

"The old pews gave the audience a sense of togetherness, of community. But I've got to admit the new seats are a lot easier on the butt." They shared a comradely laugh. "People don't fidget as much, especially during a long play. So you see, you get something, you lose something," he added philosophically.

They continued down the aisle. "The dressing rooms are over there—" Andy pointed to a space beyond the stage left wings "—in the old sacristy. The stage was once the chancel, conveniently framed by that gorgeous stone archway. All we had to do was build the stage floor up to the highest level."

"It's a wonderful theater," Joy said. There was an inherent tranquility in the space that she had missed before. But with the nerves and tension of the audition behind her, she sensed it strongly now, as she saw Andy's determination to respect and preserve it.

"You're going to enjoy being here," he said, his voice full of quiet promise.

"I think I am," she agreed.

He led the way across to the stage right wings and down a metal circular staircase. The basement housed the theater's shops, large rooms where sets and costumes were built, lighting equipment readied and repaired, properties stored. It was dank and bare, permeated by the penetrating reek of paint and sawdust. Obviously, Joy thought as she wrinkled her nose, the sprucing-up money hadn't gone as far as the basement.

At first glance the set shop looked like a corral. Sawhorses stood every which way on the cement floor like a herd of animals grazing in the sawdust. A dark muscular man with a slight paunch stood next to a door flat, scraping away infinitesimal bits of wood from the jamb with a hand plane.

Gretchen steadied the flat as he worked. "I was starting to think you'd rushed off to do something else," she said to Andy as he and Joy walked over to the flat. "He does that all the time," she remarked to Joy with proprietary concern. "Drives me crazy."

Ignoring Gretchen's comment, Andy introduced Joy to the carpenter, Larry Garvin. Larry explained briefly why he'd made the change in the door and how it worked. Andy tried it a couple of times, slammed it once hard, then jiggled the supports. "Good work, Larry," he said. "You'd better change the marks for the desk, Gretch. Move 'em out a couple of inches so there's not such a squeeze to get to the door. But make sure I look at it before you call the half hour. And get Alice to run through her exit."

Gretchen made a couple of notes on her clipboard. "Okay."

"Shall we finish our tour?" he said to Joy, and started to leave the room.

"Don't forget to call Mary Petersen at the state arts council," Gretchen reminded him. "She's expecting to hear from you before five."

"Right," he said with a snap of his fingers. "Just time to show you the parish house before I go back to the office."

"How do you keep everything straight?" Joy asked as she followed Andy up the spiral staircase.

"That's why I have Gretchen," he replied. "Most organized human being I ever met."

He led her out a rear door and into a large garden that extended behind the rambling house next to the theater. The grass was brown, the trees bare, the flower beds choked with decaying leaves, but even in its winter disrepair it awakened a longing in Joy. "You sure don't get anything like this in New York," she remarked. Of course there was Central Park and the many pocket parks that sprouted gamely between the tall buildings like grass between cobblestones, but none of those green spaces were just outside her door. She tramped across the lawn behind Andy, listening to the crunch of the ice-stiff blades of grass beneath their feet. *What a welcome change from hard concrete and harsh city sounds*, she thought.

"Only one of the many reasons why I live here and not there," Andy said. They mounted three rickety wooden steps to a small porch. "This is the parish house, now our dormitory, dining hall and general meeting place." They entered a big old-fashioned kitchen. The appliances were all vintage models and the linoleum floor was worn through to the boards in places, but it was warm and tidy. Potted plants crowded the windowsills and spilled over to shelves, the top of the fridge, cabinets and counters.

"Who keeps things so neat?" Joy asked. She'd lived in enough communal situations in summer stock and at other regional theaters to expect a certain amount of chaos.

"One of the house rules. Neatness counts. And we have Mrs. Cohen," he added.

"Who's that?" Joy asked as she wandered into the dining room.

"Our adopted grandmother." He leaned comfortably in the doorway, watching Joy circle the room. "She comes in everyday to straighten up and cook lunch. Everybody pays into a grocery kitty, and we add enough to give Mrs. Cohen a small salary. Residents kick in a bit more to keep the kitchen stocked with breakfast foods."

Joy straightened one of the many mismatched place mats that dotted the massive, scarred dining table and pushed in one of a motley assortment of chairs that surrounded it. "All the comforts of home," she said with a happy smile. The other times she'd worked out of town she'd stayed in cramped apartments or a rented room, once even a run-down motel. This would be like moving in with a family for a couple of months. The Arc's parish house would never end up on the pages of *House Beautiful*, but it sure beat that motel room. She laughed aloud.

"What's so funny?" Andy asked, catching a contagious chuckle.

She told him about the motel. "It had singing plumbing. Every time you ran water or flushed, the pipes delivered an operatic aria. I guess it was the air or something. Sometimes we'd come back from the show and open all the taps and flush all the johns at the same time to see if we could get the pipes to sing in harmony. One of the guys would stand out in back of the motel below the row of bathroom windows and coordinate. Closing night we got a perfect four-note chord." By the time she got to the end of her story, she was laughing so hard she had to hold on to the nearest chair for support. "I hadn't thought about that for ages."

Andy laughed along with her, enjoying her merriment as much as the story itself. "You have a great laugh," he said. "I like the way it sounds—full and rich."

"Yeah?" She looked up at him and met his eyes; a laserlike beam of understanding connected them, sending a current of energy and light coursing between them, growing stronger with each pulse.

"Yeah," he said softly. He paused and then said with a nod of his head, "Come on, let me show you that room."

The front bedroom on the second floor was furnished with two single beds, two dressers, two desks. The only thing that matched was the blue-flowered comforters on the beds. But sun streamed in through the bay windows and reflected colored light off the stained glass transom on the door. "Would I have to share?" she asked.

"I don't think so, but you'd better check with Gretchen to be sure."

"Linen included?" she said practically, though her mind would much rather have strayed to more pleasant thoughts, thoughts that were almost exclusively about Andy Thornhill.

"Blankets and pillows. You're on your own for sheets and towels. There's a Laundromat around the corner."

She tested the beds, first with her hand and then bouncing lightly on one of them. "I'll take it," she decided. "But only because the price is right."

"You won't be sorry, little lady," he said, imitating the greasy voice of a used-car salesman. Then he turned serious. "I'm sure you won't be. And I don't just mean the room. I have a very good feeling about you being here."

"Me, too, Andy," she replied quietly.

They went back downstairs and out through the kitchen, stopping to say hello to one of the actors in the current production who had just come in. She liked everything she had seen that afternoon—from the theater itself to the parish house to the way Andy interacted with his staff. He was clearly in charge, but he was no tyrant playing power games and using people as pawns. Then she remembered feeling like a bullied recruit during her audition.

"One more stop," he was saying. "My digs." He pointed to a small building at the back of the garden, built of the same gray granite blocks as the church. "Also the office. I can make that phone call and you can fill out the paperwork, social security number and all that. We'll have your contract ready by Monday."

As they trooped across the yard, she said, "Before I sign on the dotted line I'd like to say that I didn't much like playing buck private to your crusty sergeant this afternoon." Hard as it was to say her piece, she felt it was better to get things out in the open, clear them up, not let them grow and fester.

"You may not have liked it, but it worked, didn't it?"

"Yes," she admitted, "but it put me off."

They reached the carriage house, and he held open the door for her. "Joy, when I'm in that theater all I care about is putting together the best production I possibly can. I don't try to hurt anyone's feelings, but frankly I'm not concerned with personal feelings then. I'm concerned with getting the best results I can. How you feel is your problem. I'm sorry if that seems callous, but I'd never get through half of *this*—" he gestured around the script- and paper-filled room "—much less everything else that needs to be done if I had to play nursemaid to people's feelings, too."

"I just wanted to be clear about something that was bothering me. I didn't ask for a nursemaid," she retorted.

"If I thought you needed one I wouldn't be giving you these." He pulled a set of forms from a file drawer and handed them to her. "And I understand why you had to say what you did."

"And I understand that I'll probably want to strangle you during rehearsals now and then," she said lightly.

"And if I'm very lucky you'll restrain yourself." He chuckled and grinned broadly at her. "I'm glad we had this little chat. We understand each other much better now." Blithely he snatched the phone from the larger of the two desks in the room and tugged at the long extension cord coiled on the floor. "While you fill those out, I'll make my call and put the kettle on for tea." He cradled the receiver on his shoulder and walked into the other room, punching in the number in rhythm with his steps.

Joy sat at the smaller of the two desks—Gretchen's, judging by the neatness—and filled out the simple forms. By contrast, Andy's desk was piled high with scripts, opened books, sketches, stacks of file folders, directories and a number of half-used yellow legal pads. There were scripts and books crammed into every shelf and piles of unopened manila envelopes—submissions, she surmised, from aspiring playwrights—stacked on the floor beside the filing cabinets. She heard the kettle whistle sharply, and in a couple of minutes Andy came back into the office.

"Tea's on," he said, and replaced the phone on the desk.

She followed him into the spacious back room, simply furnished and surprisingly free of clutter. There was a red-toned rya rug on the polished wood floor, a sectional sofa covered in a rough tweed, a black leather recliner flanked by a reading light. The coffee table held an earthenware teapot and mugs, a bowl of apples and a plate of cheese and crackers.

"I'm not sure I had lunch today," he said as he sat with her on the sofa.

"I know I didn't," Joy replied. She'd been too nervous to eat, and gratefully accepted a cracker and chunk of cheddar. While he poured the tea, she said, "This room is quite a change from the office. I'm surprised to see the paperwork hasn't taken over in here, too."

He laughed dryly. "It's not because it doesn't try. The stuff seems to reproduce like rabbits. But I make a real effort to keep my living quarters private. I may bring a script in here to read or work on, but it doesn't stay here overnight. Unless I fall asleep over it," he added sheepishly. He felt a tug of longing when he thought of the too many nights he had spent in this room curled up with a script. It sure didn't keep him warm at night— the way she would.

"I noticed that pile of unopened scripts," she said with a shake of her head. "All those people's hopes and dreams, stuffed into an envelope, waiting to get out. So many of them. You could probably stay awake every night from now till July and not read them all. I don't know how you keep up. I've only been here a couple of hours and I'm tired from watching you."

"If you want something badly enough you find a way to have it."

They were silent for a moment, and Joy thought about how close she was to something she wanted very much. But wanting and having were two different things. Having a job at the Arc would be easy to accept; her growing feelings for Andy Thornhill less so.

"Why don't you stay for the performance tonight?" he asked suddenly, and laid a light finger on the back of her hand.

Her skin bristled as a shiver of anticipation somersaulted down her neck. "I'd like that," she answered, despite her misgivings. What harm could it do to see a show in the theater where she'd be performing in a matter of weeks? The only harm would come if she let her attraction to Andy get the better of her.

"Good. So would I." He swigged the last of his tea and stood up. "I've got to get over to the theater. You can stay here and relax for a while. Or," he said with a mischievous smile, "you could read through a few of those scripts."

She laughed merrily. "Never a dull moment around here, I see."

"I should hope not," he said with mock indignation. "Gotta run. See you at the theater in an hour." He grabbed an apple and rushed out the door.

The room seemed unusually quiet and still after he'd gone. Joy closed her eyes and savored the silence, enjoying the pleasant tiredness that came after exertion and excitement. She was far from spent, though; she was merely recharging her batteries. Five minutes later she went into the office, plucked a couple of envelopes from the top of the pile and picked up a pad and pencil from Andy's desk. Back in the living room she kicked off her shoes, switched on the reading lamp and settled comfortably into the recliner.

4

"JOY?"

She heard Andy's voice in the outer room and stuck her pen in the script to mark her place. "Hi."

He paused in the doorway between the two rooms. "Don't you look right at home," he said, both pleased and amused by how natural it seemed to see her reading in the recliner.

As soon as she'd settled into the chair to read, she'd realized how quickly she'd become attuned to the rhythms of the place. Being in Andy's room was comfortable, so comfortable it made her a bit wary that she was traveling too far too quickly into a world, however familiar it seemed, that she knew too little about. The feeling itself had surprised her, but his awareness of it did not. "I have this funny sense that I belong here," she told him. "It started this afternoon in the parish house. I'm usually not too comfortable in new surroundings. It's strange."

"Maybe. Maybe not. Everybody has a niche. The trick is in finding it. You ready to go? Curtain's in fifteen minutes."

Joy jumped up and stepped into her shoes. "Is it that late already?" She dropped the script on the chair, but then remembered Andy's efforts to keep his living space clear of theater work. "Oops," she said, and they exchanged a smile. She picked it up again and on the way out put it on his desk. "I took some notes and left them in the front of the book," she told him as he helped her into her coat.

"Good. I'll look at them later. Play any good?" The yard was dark and the grass had turned icy, and he took her arm as they crossed to the theater.

"Not bad. But it didn't give me goose pimples."

"Is that the Kingsley rating system? Number of goose pimples per act? What's it take for a hit? Twenty-five per square inch of skin?"

"Twenty-five's only good for a limited run," she scoffed lightly. "I'd say you need at least forty for a hit."

"Tough critic," he said, squeezing her arm and pulling her closer and slightly off balance. Joy's right foot buckled, and she clung to him, afraid she was falling farther than just onto the grass. He stopped her skid, and as she righted herself she felt his warm breath on her cheeks: "Okay?" he asked.

"I think so," she said, her breath forming white clouds of condensation as fluttery as the quivering in her solar plexus.

They continued on into the theater, and Andy guided her down the hall past the dressing rooms to a door that led to the auditorium. "I reserved a house seat for you. Tell the usher on the center aisle who you are. I'll meet you here after the show." He pressed her hand quickly and hurried away.

Joy was shown to her seat and given a program. She was usually an avid reader of programs, especially the short biographies—she liked to know the actors' credits, to look for connections between the jobs they had, to know about the director, the playwright and the designers who had worked on the show. But tonight she was more interested in surveying the audience, for in four short weeks a similar group of people would assemble to see a play in which she would be acting one of the two leading roles. It was a diverse group—students and tweedy faculty types from the nearby University of Pennsylvania; well-heeled couples from the suburbs; a dozen or so senior citizens sitting together, probably a club outing; lots of "young urban professionals." They were lively and animated, not as blasé or jaded as an off-Broadway audience, nor as frivolous as a dinner theater or summer stock crowd, but somewhere in between—interested and alert, but still out to have fun. A good group to play to, she decided, receptive but not pushovers.

The houselights dimmed, and she soon found herself immersed in *Bananas Over You*. In the tradition of all farce, it was highly dependent on the opening and closing of doors. A sticky door, like the one that had been fixed that afternoon, could throw off the delicate timing, slow the momentum and kill the laughs. The new door was working well, and by the end of the final act Joy's stomach hurt from laughing too much. And her admiration for Andy's talent and the quality of the Arc company had grown even more.

She stayed in her seat as the audience filed out, listening to their comments. "Didn't you love it when . . ." and "I thought I'd die laughing when . . ." and "Didn't that scene remind you of . . ." Their faces were happy, expressive and relaxed. They had been reached and affected by the performance, just as she had. The house emptied, and the ushers began to collect the discarded programs and put up the seats. The young woman she had seen in the box office that afternoon appeared onstage to collect the props. Even in the empty theater Joy thought she could hear laughter echoing off the vaulted ceiling, as if the energy in the room hadn't entirely dissipated.

She waited another ten minutes until the theater began to grow chilly before she went backstage to look for Andy. A round of raucous laughs rose from one of the dressing rooms, and she walked down the hall toward it. The cast was assembled in the men's dressing room, perched on counters, sitting two to a chair or cross-legged on the floor, listening to Andy's comments on the performance.

"Great impulse, Alice," he complimented. He described a bit of business that had been especially funny. Joy had assumed it had been rehearsed, but from what Andy was saying she learned it had developed spontaneously that night. "Keep it in." There was a good-natured groan from the actor at whose expense the gesture was aimed.

"Just you wait, Alice," the actor vowed.

Joy hung back in the hall outside the door until Andy and then Gretchen had run down the list of notes they had compiled during the performance. As Gretchen was speaking, Andy caught sight of Joy and flashed her an effervescent smile. The moment business was concluded he slipped out of the room.

He draped an arm around Joy's shoulders and shepherded her down the hall. "I hope you don't mind if I'm selfish and whisk you off alone. You can meet everyone next week. Enjoy the show?"

"It was great. I'm impressed," she allowed, welcoming the weight of his touch as they crossed the yard to the carriage house.

"And I'm starving," he said, evidently satisfied with her answer. "Can I take you out for the best meal in Philly?"

"That sounds like an offer neither I nor my rumbling stomach could refuse."

"Just let me grab a jacket." He rushed inside and came out wearing a burnt orange down parka. He pulled a pair of wool gloves out of the pockets. "Car's parked in front of the parish house," he said.

Soon they had left West Philadelphia and were cruising down the Schuylkill Expressway in Andy's middle-aged green Volvo. Once off the highway, they drove down a series of narrow one-way streets lined on both sides with tight ranks of row houses. They passed an empty softball field, and Andy pulled up in front of a long, skinny whitewashed building. A wide over-hang fitted with garish yellow fluorescent lights covered the sidewalk all around it. Despite the cold, knots of people, mostly adolescent boys, huddled on the sidewalk.

"Welcome to Anthony's," Andy said, "or as we say here in Sout' Philly—Ant-neeze."

"It sounds like you're talking about the joints on certain insects' legs," Joy said with a laugh.

"This is some joint all right," Andy rejoined.

It looked dubious, but if Andy said it was good she was willing to give it a try. She put her hand on the door handle, but he reached out to stop her. "Aren't we going in?" she asked.

"There is no in. This is it. Unless you'd prefer the sidewalk or a table alfresco." He pointed to a couple of molded plastic picnic tables in an eye-boggling shade of magenta.

Though the color was hot, she could imagine how cold the plastic would be in this weather. "This table is fine, waiter," she said gamely. "I think I'll start with the pâté de foie gras and have the stuffed quail for the main course."

"Of course, madam." He looked down at an imaginary pad and read back the order. "That's two cheese steaks. With or without?"

"With or without what? And what's a cheese steak?"

"Onions. And you'll find out what a cheese steak is in a minute. Want to come with me?"

"Sure. I might as well have the whole experience, including the onions." She hopped out of the car and skipped around to meet him on the sidewalk.

Through a barely opened glass window, Andy gave their order to one of the three men behind the grill inside the small kitchen. "Two cheese with," he said. "Two fries, one with cheese and—" he turned to Joy to ask what she wanted to drink "—two ginger ales."

The cooks in their spattered white aprons all had ballooning bellies, presumably inflated from sampling the wares, but that didn't hamper the largest man's speed in grilling thin slices of steak, flipping them onto a long Italian roll and ladling melted cheese and a spatula full of fried onions on top. Another filled two paper boats with fried shoestring potatoes and topped one with a dollop of the same melted cheese. The third drew the sodas from the fountain. Beside the window there was a row of glass jars, the kind that hold nuts and candies in candy stores, and Joy and Andy loaded up on ketchup and hot peppers.

Back in the car they balanced their feast precariously on the dashboard and dug in. Joy started with her sandwich, bit through the crusty roll, felt the tang of the ketchup on the tip of her tongue, the squish of the melted cheese, the sweetness of the onions and finally hit the rich grilled beef. She chewed slowly, letting all the tastes and textures mingle in her mouth. "Mmmm. Now I know why you're so keen on Philadelphia. It has nothing to do with the theater at all."

"Told you it was the best meal in town. Taste one of these." He plucked a cheese-covered fry from the paper boat and fed it to her.

It was gooey and greasy and sinfully delicious. "Classic American cuisine," she said approvingly, and plucked another fry from the dish. "But seriously, how did you end up in Philly?"

"I grew up here, out in the suburbs, got my undergraduate degree at the University of Pennsylvania. I came home one weekend while I was still studying for my Masters in Fine Art at Yale and came into town to visit a friend who was at law school at Penn. We were walking around West Philadelphia and passed this boarded-up church. 'That would make a great theater,' I said. I hadn't even thought about it. The idea just popped out. My buddy and I poked around the place for a few minutes, and I started to see the genuine possibilities. And to get excited." He nibbled on a plain fry and took a sip of soda. "I asked one of my brothers to find out about the property. It had reverted to the city in lieu of taxes, so I started a campaign to get them to rent it to me. I made such a pest of myself that eventually they did."

"And now you've turned a derelict building into a valuable city asset."

"Yeah," he said with an ironic laugh, "and the guys at city hall who gave me such a hard time are now crowing about their foresightedness."

"You're pretty cynical," Joy observed.

"No, just realistic. A lot of the people I went to graduate school with went straight to New York. Eight years

later too many of them haven't worked six months in a
row. I didn't want that. I wanted to work, to do what I
was trained to do, what I love to do. And I have. I'm
only thirty-two, but I've already made a contribu-
tion—a lasting one I hope—to the theater. I have a
dream, Joy, and day by day I'm making it come true."

"We all have dreams, Andy," she said quietly. There
was a fierceness, a determination about him that was
disconcerting at times.

"What's yours?" he asked.

"To move people in the theater, make 'em laugh and
cry, to act great roles."

"Where do you see yourself in five years?"

She nibbled at her sandwich and thought. "Working
steadily, known to producers and directors, sought
after."

"In New York?"

"Mostly. And what about you? Where do you see
yourself in five years?"

"Here. At the Arc," he answered promptly, defini-
tively.

"Will it be big enough for you in five years, even next
year?"

He looked at her sharply. "Why wouldn't it be?"

"You do good work, Andy. I thought you might want
to let the rest of the world in on it," she said gently.

He finished his sandwich and crumpled the wax paper wrapping into a tight ball. "My sister-in-law told
me a wonderful story a couple of weeks ago. Her son,
my nephew David—he's eight—was playing at their
house with a friend. The friend said to David, 'I wonder what it's like in outer space.' Dave thought for a
minute and then answered, 'You know, we *are* in outer

space.' You see? We're all so worried about what's 'out there' we don't realize that there is here."

Joy chuckled appreciatively. "I get the point. But it doesn't preclude the possibility that there *is* something more 'out there.'"

"Hey," Andy said, "how did we get into all this heavy stuff?"

"Let's see." She thought back to the start of the conversation. "All I did was ask you how you ended up in Philadelphia. I thought it was just because of Ant-neeze cheese steaks, but then you—"

He tweaked her playfully on the nose. "Forget all that other malarkey I told you. It's only because of Ant-neeze. Want to split another sandwich? I'm still hungry."

"I couldn't," she declared, then changed her mind. "Aw, what the heck, why not?"

"That's the spirit. Be right back."

What a day, Joy thought. *Twelve hours ago I was walking to Penn Station on my way to an audition and now I'm parked on a street corner eating fried beef and arguing with Andy Thornhill about the meaning of life.* It sure didn't take long to turn things upside down, she considered wryly.

Andy jumped back into the car and slammed the door against the freezing air. "I'm not being a very good host," he said as he handed her half the steaming sandwich. "I completely forgot the music. We're supposed to be listening to golden oldies. It's all part of the experience." He turned on the radio and twisted the dial. "It's all your fault. You make me forget things, Joy." He looked at her intently. "You know that?"

She felt herself getting as gushy and gooey as the cheese on her sandwich and gave an ambiguous shake

of her head in answer. She wasn't sure how much she
wanted him to forget, especially since they'd be working together for the next two months.

"Ah, here we go." He tuned into a station playing
"Sixteen Candles" and sang along for a couple of lines.
Joy joined in, and soon they were crooning at the top
of their lungs and giggling as if they were sixteen again.
When they quieted down, they noticed a trio of teen-
agers huddled beside the car looking in at them as if
they were truly weird, which launched them into even
larger gales of laughter.

Andy gave the kids a scram sign with his thumb, and
they slunk off. "Now if we really want to give them their
money's worth we could . . ." He clapped his sandwich
on the dash and wrapped one arm around her shoulders. Quickly his lips closed on hers.

The kiss took her by surprise, like an unexpected
twist of plot in a film or play. At first she was delighted
and amused by the impetuous gesture, but when he
deepened the kiss, held her more tightly, more insis-
tently, she tensed. The script was moving too fast, a
scene or two had been glossed over or cut out completely.

She pulled away from him and rested her head
against the seat. She had tasted so many new things today, not that she hadn't liked her first tantalizing taste
of his lips, but she was approaching sensory overload.
Another jolt like the last and her circuits could break.

As she recovered and breathed easier, she became
aware that her hands were uncomfortably greasy and
warm. She looked down at her lap to see that she had
gripped her sandwich so hard while he was kissing her
that the filling had run out over her hands and onto the
waxed paper. She made a small groan, and Andy

looked down. When he raised his eyes to hers, they both broke up. *This is better*, she thought. *Light and easy is how it should be now.*

"You can dress me up," she joked, "but you can't take me out."

"Honestly," he said with feigned vexation. Then he lifted one of her hands and seemed about to deliver a playful slap to it, but instead brought it to his lips and slowly licked all five fingers clean. By the time he started on the other hand, her breath was coming in small, irregular gasps, part laughter, part exquisite pleasure.

"Stop," she pleaded.

"I can't. We don't have enough napkins."

"You're crazy." She pulled her hand away and reached onto the dashboard for a paper napkin.

"Only about you."

"Don't you think we should slow down? We've only known each other a few hours."

"So what? I have the same feeling about you that I had when I first saw the church, Joy. A feeling of infinite possibilities."

She wrapped up the remains of the crushed sandwich and put it in one of the empty French-fry boats. "It's getting late, Andy. Maybe I'd better see about catching a train."

He looked wounded as he cupped her face with his hands. "Don't change the subject. I just said something very important to you."

"I'm sorry. I didn't know how to respond."

"You liked kissing me, didn't you?"

"Yes."

"And being with me today and the other night?"

"Yes."

"So what's the problem? You're doing it again, Joy, you're worried about 'out there.' Be here, be here with me. Now. Please."

His voice was tender, full of yearning. With infinite care, he touched her lips with his, kissed her lightly, briefly. Even so tenuous a touch elicited that too strong magnetic pull she felt toward him.

"I don't want to take you to the train, Joy. I want you to stay with me tonight. Let me love you. . . ."

"Hey, hold the phone there," she said, struggling to keep her voice airy. "Haven't you skipped a couple of scenes?"

Damn, Andy swore silently, *I'm doing it again. She gets under my skin so easily that I'm rushing things, trying to get from the beginning to the end and leaving out the middle.* "Yeah, I guess I have." He sat back and ran his hand through his hair. They were both silent, allowing the tension to pass. When the air seemed clear, he leaned forward and grinned at her. "I hope you'll consider this an open invitation."

"I'll keep it in mind," she said. She couldn't resist his smile any more than she wanted to close off any avenues with him. She just wanted to walk down them more slowly.

"We should get going." He gathered up the refuse, stepped out of the car, dumped it in the nearest trash bin and got back in. "I'll come into the station with you," he said as he started up the car. "Make sure there is a train."

They drove silently down dark, mostly deserted streets. Except for a couple of taxis, Andy's was the only car at the Thirtieth Street Station curb. Inside the stately old depot their footsteps rang roundly on the marble floor. Joy felt the reverberations of every move inside her head. Everything seemed magnified, out of proportion now. She needed time and private space to digest the events of the long, stressful and taxing day.

The departures board showed that the last express was scheduled to leave in ten minutes. "Just in the nick of time," Andy said with a frown. They started toward the escalator to go down to the designated platform. "I'm sorry you're not staying, but I understand why you have to go."

"I'm glad *you* do," she said with an uneasy laugh. She knew she'd made the right decision, but now that the moment of parting was at hand the passionate, spontaneous part of her was warring with the sensible side in a way that was new and disconcerting.

"Want me to explain it to you?"

"Nah, it'll give me something to think about on the train."

"I should have slipped a couple of scripts in your purse. At least you'd have had something constructive to do."

"Thinking isn't constructive?"

"Thinking yes, brooding no."

The few people on the platform were weary-looking and subdued, talking in whispers if at all. The darkness of the surrounding tunnels and the late hour were conducive to silence, and Andy seemed content to wait quietly for the announcement and the clanging bell that would precede the train's arrival. But a single clear thought navigated its way to the shores of Joy's brain.

"You know I'm not playing coy or hard to get?" she asked.

"Neither am I," he said with a smile and a raise of his eyebrows.

"So I noticed." She also noticed how his smile sent her pulse racing.

The public address system crackled loudly, and the New York train was announced. At the end of the platform the train's headlight rounded into the tunnel.

"So. I'll see you Monday morning," Andy said above the ca-lang, ca-lang of the bell and the approaching roar of the engine.

"I'll probably come down on Sunday afternoon to get settled."

"Good, I'll see you then," he said. The train pulled up, and they moved a couple of steps toward the nearest door. "Take care, Joy." He reached out, brushed her cheek lightly and stepped back, trying to make it easier for himself to let her go.

When the doors had opened and the departing passengers had disembarked, she found it hard to move away from him. Her brain tugged her forward into the train and her heart tugged her back. But she willed herself to step past the conductor and into the train. "G'night," she said softly, and disappeared into the carriage.

She found an empty seat and huddled next to the window, trying to look ahead to the busy weekend she would have and not back on the unsettling evening. She pulled a pen and paper out of her bag and began to make a list of all the things she had to do before leaving. There would be no time to sublet her apartment, and it was hardly worth it for two months, but she'd have to ask someone, maybe Steven across the hall, to water the plants and forward her mail. Then there was the dry cleaning, laundry. She had to notify her answering service and the restaurant, pack, cancel appointments.

The list was far from complete, but it wasn't absorbing enough to stop her mind from replaying the scenes of the day. They all ran together like one of those paintings she had made at carnivals as a kid—drops of vividly colored paint swirled into an abstract design by a whirling machine. She looked at the painting from different angles, trying to consider its many possibilities, its "infinite possibilities," to use Andy's phrase.

ANDY DIDN'T WAIT for the train to leave. He turned on his heels and took the stairs of the escalator two at a time, as if speed would help him feel her absence less. After today his impulse toward her was even stronger. It was the same kind of feeling he'd had when he saw the church for the first time. *And look where that impulse led you. But people aren't empty buildings,* he told himself. *You can't take them apart and put them back together to suit yourself.*

That didn't mean, Andy decided as he hurried to the car, that he couldn't hold on to the dream he'd already formed about her, that he couldn't try to make it come true. If he hadn't stuck to his instincts about the theater, he'd never be where he was today. It was the same process, but the technique needed refining, he concluded. Revving the engine hard, he pulled out into the traffic and headed for home.

5

A FEW MINUTES BEFORE TEN on Monday morning, carrying script and a pencil, Joy crossed the yard from the parish house to the stage door of the theater. She paused before opening the door and closed her eyes briefly, a symbolic gesture to mark her entry. Once she was inside, the world of the play would take precedence, and she needed the moment's pause to leave everything else behind.

The stage was lit with a couple of work lights, just enough power to enable the actors to see their scripts. The furniture from the romantic farce, which would continue to play for the first three weeks of rehearsal, had been moved into the wings. A semicircle of folding chairs ringed center stage.

The other five cast members had already arrived and were chatting among themselves. She recognized two who were in the cast of the farce. Two others were strangers, and the fifth, Ken Dreiser, she had met the previous evening when she had arrived at the parish house. He was also from New York, but unlike her had worked frequently at the Arc. The other four lived in or near Philadelphia and were also Arc regulars.

Joy said good morning to Ken—tall, powerful, energetic, with a craggy face and a thick thatch of salt-and-pepper hair. He looked rather like she imagined a gentleman farmer of the nineteenth century would look—no stranger to hard physical work but refined and cultured as well. Not exactly the type she had imagined for the role of Barbara's mercurial father, but doubtless chosen by Andy for good reason.

"I heard something suspiciously like an exercise tape at half past seven this morning as I passed your room," he said.

Joy laughed. "You're a fine one to talk. You were on your way in from running. I saw you go out."

"Ugh," came a groan from the woman standing beside Ken. She was in her mid-forties, with a rather plain face marked by strong features and vibrant brown eyes. "How can you even talk about exercising at that hour? I can barely grope my way to a cup of coffee then." She extended her hand to Joy. "Sarah Brock—your wicked half sister. If in fact you're our Barbara."

Sarah smiled, and Joy saw just how deceptive the plainness was. Her face was the sort that took beauty from the harsh stage lights instead of washing out as prettier, less distinctive women often did. With makeup and her auburn hair released from the barrette that held it back, she would make a considerable impression on stage. Joy introduced herself and shook Sarah's hand. In the handclasp she felt Sarah taking measure of her, felt the strength of her formidable presence. She would be someone to reckon with, onstage and off.

As she and Sarah were shaking hands, Ken assumed the role of host and gathered the three secondary members of the cast for introductions. Lila Callahan would play both her and Sarah's mother in the flashbacks. Mark Curran was her husband and Harvey Winston was Sarah's. The round of friendly hellos was just completed when Andy made his entrance.

"Good morning, people. Glad to see you all." He slapped Mark and Harvey on the back as he passed them. "Joy and Ken, I hope you're settled. If there's anything else you need, complain to Gretchen," he said breezily as he shook Ken's hand.

"Thanks a lot," chimed in Gretchen, who had just hurried onstage. "It's not easy being the person where the buck always stops," she responded to the general chuckling.

Andy and Sarah kissed each other on both cheeks; Lila got a warm two-handed shake and a gallant bow. He stopped in front of Joy and met her eyes squarely. "Welcome to the Arc," he said formally. He'd made up his mind over the weekend to slow the tempo of the music that flooded his veins whenever he saw or thought about her. Despite his intentions his pulse dictated the rhythm, and it was rapid, racing now, as he faced her. "I take it you've met everyone."

She nodded. They hadn't seen each other since the train station on Friday night. Pictures of that evening exploded in her mind, popping like a string of firecrackers. He only needed to be close to her to spark a chain reaction. *Please don't touch me*, she warned him with her eyes. *Not here, not now.*

"Good," he said, after a moment. "Then we can get started." He stepped back from the group to the edge of the stage. "Take a seat. It doesn't matter where. Just make sure you can see everyone else. We'll read through the first act from the top, including the short stage directions. If it's a long piece about set or character, Gretchen will take it. No acting, please. Forget whatever choices you made for your auditions. Forget what I said to you when you read for me. Today we start to find out together what the play is about. Take as much time as you need."

He said a few words to Gretchen, hopped off the stage and took a seat in the audience. Gretchen stayed onstage with the actors but moved her chair outside the semicircle. Sarah and Ken took the two center chairs. Joy sat next to Ken; Lila next to Sarah; Mark and Harvey in the end seats. They adjusted their chairs for sight lines, then riffled through their scripts to find the beginning of act one. When everyone was settled, they looked to Gretchen to begin, but she remained silent. Gradually, as the actors became calmer, stopped fidgeting entirely, a hush settled over the theater. Andy signaled to Gretchen. The rehearsal began.

They had a break after reading act one, and Andy rushed off to the office. Joy spent the fifteen minutes quietly thinking about what they had read, letting her mind wander. The others chatted intermittently; Sarah and Harvey went off to the parish house for coffee. When Andy returned after the recess, they read the second act of the play in the same way as the first, and then without comment from the director adjourned to the parish house for lunch.

Mark Curran walked with her to the house. He was playing the romantic lead in the farce but was far from a typical leading man. He was small, with dull brown hair and a genteel round face that wore a perpetual air of mild astonishment. "How do you like the theater so far?" he asked.

"Terrific," Joy answered. "Especially having lunch laid on for you. No scrambling off and bolting something down in order to get back on time. It reminds me of going home for lunch when I was a kid."

"Wait until you meet Mrs. Cohen. It *is* like going home for lunch."

They entered the kitchen behind Harvey and Lila, and immediately a bursting bubble of a lady bounced up to Joy. "You must be the new girl," she cried. "It's so nice to meet you. Tell me your name, darling." Joy did, and she clapped her hands together. "What a nice name, and I bet it's your own. You don't look like the kind of girl who would change her name. That's one thing I don't like about this theater business. It's like those nose jobs. I don't like people who have them, either. A nose is a nose is a nose," she proclaimed.

Joy and Mark exchanged barely concealed grins with Harvey and Lila. Mrs. Cohen forged ahead undaunted. She put an ample arm around Joy and steered her toward the dining room. "You're very pretty, darling, but too thin. All the girls are too thin these days. In my day a man wanted zaftig, juicy, a little something to pinch, to keep him warm at night."

"Plenty warm I kept my Arnold," came a chorus from behind them.

Mrs. Cohen turned around and faced the laughing group. "All right, you smarty-pantses, wait until you're seventy-two. You'll repeat yourselves more than once, too. Now eat the soup before it gets cold." She smiled benignly at all of them and bustled back into the kitchen.

The group lined up to ladle bowls of mushroom and barley soup from a large pot and help themselves to cold cuts, cheese, bread and salad. Joy had just sat down when she heard Mrs. Cohen say from the kitchen, "Well, if it isn't Mr. Hustle and Bustle himself come to grace us with his presence."

"Just came to grab a quick sandwich, Mrs. C.," Andy said.

"Sit and eat," she commanded. "You'll get an ulcer the way you eat and run."

Andy entered the dining room, prodded from behind by Mrs. C. "All these nice people here, our beautiful new Joy, and you can't take fifteen minutes for a meal. What's more important?" He threw up his arms in surrender and sat beside Joy.

"I thought you said you ran this place," Joy said under her breath.

"Even Napoleon had a grandmother," he replied. While everyone was laughing, he gave her a small private smile that told her she wasn't the only one to remember what had happened between them on Friday night. Then he dug into the bowl of soup Mrs. Cohen had put in front of him.

Joy spread mustard on a piece of rye bread and topped it with a slice of Swiss cheese, feeling happier, more alive than she had in months. She saw the next eight weeks strung ahead of her like Christmas lights, each waiting to be turned on, to burn a different bright color.

Andy bolted down his soup, slapped together a sandwich and said to the group, "I hate to deprive you of my company, but I've got critics to court."

"What are you hanging around here for then?" Sarah asked, waving her hand as if to shoo him from the room. He winked at them all, let his eyes fall lingeringly on Joy and was gone.

Joy finished her lunch, chatting with her fellow cast members and two of the farce players who had just wandered into the dining room. They were on loose daytime schedules now that their show was up and running. Afterward she went for a short walk to get some fresh air and a few rays of the weak January sun before returning to the theater.

In the afternoon they reconvened—without Gretchen who had more pressing duties—and read through act one much more slowly. Andy sat on the stage with them, and they stopped frequently to discuss the play's themes and the issues facing each character. At five-thirty, earlier than scheduled, Andy dismissed them. "That's a good day's work, people. See you all in the morning. And, Joy, can I see you in the office now?"

She covered her surprise, but not soon enough to stem a raised inquiring eyebrow from Sarah. "Sure thing," she replied, avoiding Sarah's stare. She gathered up her script and jacket and followed Andy into the yard.

"I liked the report you wrote on that script on Friday," he said. "I thought I'd try to bribe you into reading a few thousand more."

"Thanks," she said wryly. "What are you offering?"

"Cup of tea and some of Mrs. C's oatmeal cookies."

"Well," she answered with a shrug, "you already know I work cheap."

Inside he hung his jacket on a peg by the door, and Joy followed suit. "I'll get the tea. Why don't you pick through that pile of scripts? We have a theater administration student who works here a couple of mornings a week. I got Janet to open all the envelopes this morning and update the logbook."

"In anticipation of your new reader? Awfully sure of yourself, aren't you?" She started to browse through the scripts.

"Even if you hadn't volunteered it didn't do any harm to open the packages and log them in," he defended himself, but none too strenuously. "Sign out what you take in that blue spiral notebook." He settled a pleased smile on her and went through into the other room.

She picked five scripts, checked them out and left them on Andy's chair. Coming back into his neat simple room, she had the feeling she'd been there more than one brief hour. In a way she had, for all the time she'd spent there in her mind over the weekend, all the time she'd spent the previous evening wondering as she'd unpacked if she should come here, or wait for him to come to her. The ease she felt at this moment—which didn't switch off or diminish the undercurrents that flowed between them—told her she'd been right to hang back, to take things slowly with him. She moseyed into the pullman kitchen and watched him warm the teapot with hot water and spoon in loose tea from a tin caddy. "Who taught you to make tea?"

"Me auld mum," he said in a British working-class accent. "Spent a summer studying in London when I was in college."

"And majored in tea?"

"Minored in slicing lemons. Or would you prefer milk?"

"Lemon, please," she requested.

He carried the tray to the coffee table. "How'd you like the first day? I wasn't too tough, was I?" he asked as he poured out the tea.

"It was good," she said emphatically. "Until I found out I'd been conscripted." She emphasized the second syllable of the word, and they made sour faces at each other.

"Aargh," Andy said, then added, "you don't have to do it if you don't want to."

"I want to," she assured him. She nibbled at one of the spicy cookies and moved the subject away from the potentially loaded one of what other things they might want from each other. "Why did you ask us to read the stage directions this morning?"

"Because I didn't want you to ignore them—the playwright has a reason for putting them in—but I didn't want you to be tempted to act them. This is simply a way of becoming aware of them. By saying them aloud the subconscious hears them. Later, as the work gets more intense, the suggestion will be there for you to use—or not use."

"I see," she said thoughtfully, leaning back and crossing her legs. "If it's not there, you can't use it or reject it."

Andy looked at her intently; he wanted badly to take her in his arms and hold her close, so close she would be able to feel the power of the emotions that had gathered in him over the weekend. But he also wanted the warmth they were sharing now—a solid foundation for them—to grow, to build naturally. He wrapped both hands around his mug and put his attention on the thin slice of lemon, floating like a yellow barge on a lazy brown sea. "Ever been to the Caribbean?" he said, asking the first question that popped into his head.

At least I changed the subject to something relevant, Joy thought. His look, though indirect, had hardly escaped her; she'd felt it as palpably as she would a touch. "No, you seem to be the world traveler here," she replied flippantly.

"If you could go anywhere you wanted, right now, where would you go?"

"Paris," she answered without hesitation, picking up the excitement in his voice. Faster than the Concorde, her imagination put her there. "I want to take a boat down the Seine, spend days in the Louvre—"

"Andy," a voice from the outer room called, "do you know where the—" Gretchen appeared in the doorway. "Oh, sorry," she said looking flustered, as if she'd barged in on a much more intimate moment. "Have you seen that new box of gels?"

"I had Janet take them to the storeroom this morning. Want some tea?" Andy asked.

"Er, no, thanks," Gretchen said, and left without another word.

Andy seemed lost in thought for a moment, and Joy sat uneasily. Gretchen had seemed none too pleased to see her in Andy's room, she thought. But then that was Gretchen's problem. She and Andy weren't doing anything nefarious. "That was a quick trip," she said. He looked at her blankly. "Paris," she reminded him. He nodded in recognition, but didn't do anything to revive their conversation. "I'd better be going," she said after a moment of awkward silence. "Thanks for the tea. I'll get those scripts back to you as soon as I can."

"You don't have to read them all tonight."

"Don't worry. I won't. I'm going to the movies with Ken."

"A movie," Andy uttered with a far-searching look. "I saw one of those once, a long time ago."

"You should go again sometime. It's fun."

"Maybe we'll go together."

"Sure."

Andy walked her to the door and helped her into her jacket. "Take care of yourself," he said, gazing fondly at her.

She hefted the armload of scripts. "I'll try not to let anything happen between here and the house," she said lightly, not wanting him to see how his look had affected her. "See you tomorrow."

But something did happen outside. She gave in to an irresistible urge to skip across the frozen grass. *It's not just all sparks and currents between us. We have so much to share—work and tea and laughter and life at its fullest.* She looked up and sang a song of elation to the stars and twirled around and around and around till she tripped dizzily up the stairs to the back door.

DURING THE WEEK Joy settled into a pleasant routine—early-morning exercise, rehearsal, lunch, more rehearsal, tea with Andy and a couple hours' work at the Arc office sending back scripts, typing reports on plays she thought Andy should read himself. Then a quick meal, some work on her role and more reading. The more she did, the more energy she seemed to have, the more she felt capable of doing.

On Friday afternoon Andy complimented the cast on a good week's work. On Monday they'd start putting the play on its feet—getting up out of the chairs in which they'd been reading and discussing—and he asked everyone to be off book as much as possible.

Joy always looked forward to this stage of the process. Working without the encumbrance of a script allowed more freedom, both of movement and imagination. Over the week she and the rest of the cast had absorbed most of their lines through sheer repetition, and Gretchen would be there to cue them when necessary. At this point there was no need to be letter perfect, especially as the playwright would be coming in to rewrite scenes that weren't working or that needed clarification. Still, it would mean she'd need to put in a couple of hours over the weekend getting the sequence of lines straight, in addition to working on the exercises she was using to enhance her understanding of the play and her character.

The week's work successfully accomplished, the cast went their separate ways. Sarah was off to the suburbs where she lived with her husband and two teenage children; Mark and Harvey went to prepare for their performance; Lila—with strict instructions from Andy to be careful—was on her way to the Poconos to ski; Ken was taking the train to New York; Andy and Joy headed for the office.

"I'm taking the entire day off tomorrow," he announced over tea. "Gretchen's in charge for an entire twenty-four hours. Spend the day with me?"

She couldn't think of anything she'd like better and told him so. He smiled warmly at her and reached out to put his hand on hers. It was the first time he'd touched her intimately all week, and she immediately went fluttery inside, a feeling very much like stage fright, as if she were standing in the wings, waiting for the best day of her life to begin.

"Great," he said, squeezing her hand before letting it go. "Furlough begins tomorrow then. In the meantime think you can take a look at the first draft of this grant proposal?"

"I can, but I don't know anything about grant proposals."

"You will after you read this one," he told her. "I've left it on your shelf."

During the week Joy had appropriated a shelf for her scripts and reports, one more thing that gave her a sense of belonging to the place, of being a functioning part of it. It pleased her to hear him talk of it as hers, too. "I'll look at it tonight."

They worked quietly together in the office until it was time for Andy to go to the theater. "I'll come by the house tomorrow morning at ten," he said. He held her chin in his hand and brought his lips ever so briefly to rest on hers.

Joy's stomach did a pretty good imitation of an elevator with a snapped cable, plummeting precipitously and bouncing at the bottom. Her mouth went dry, and she swallowed hard. "Ten o'clock," she whispered.

6

THE WEATHER REPORT predicted snow for later in the day so Joy dressed in gray tweed pleated-front slacks, warm boots and a bulky white sweater. With her vintage navy blue British warmer, she wore a knitted Andean cap, pointed on top with earflaps and a chin strap, and matching mittens, all patterned with prancing llamas.

She was waiting in the kitchen sipping a cup of coffee when Andy arrived at the back door of the house. "Ready?" he asked quietly, knowing the other residents would only be starting to stir at this hour. She nodded and slipped into her coat, and they walked through the alley to Andy's car.

"Do we have an agenda?" she asked as he unlocked the passenger door.

"Of sorts. But it's fluid. What do you want to do?"

"See some of the city," she said. "I've been here nearly a week and I've hardly seen more than a few blocks in daylight."

"Just what I planned," he said. He opened the door, reached across to the back seat and pulled out a tricorn hat. Plunking it squarely on his head, he said, "The Benjamin Franklin Guide Service, at your service, madam. First stop, city hall."

Laughing gaily Joy got into the car, and they took off for Center City. As soon as they passed the university and went over the South Street Bridge, the scenery changed. In West Philadelphia the houses were large and rambling, semidetached with wide porches and alleyways between the pairs; the streets were broad, hilly, the trees big, with roots that often lifted sidewalks and branches that scraped porch roofs and second-floor windows. Center City houses, built in rows on narrow streets lined with tamer more gracious trees, harkened back to another age. "It's so quaint," Joy exclaimed as they drove down Pine Street. The houses were beautifully maintained, each one slightly different from its neighbor, giving a feeling of community and individuality at the same time.

At Broad Street they turned left, and Andy pulled the car over to point at the top of city hall, where William Penn kept watch over the city he had founded in 1682.

"If I wave will he wave back?" Joy asked, scrunching over to get a better view.

"You never can tell," Andy said. They both waved at Mr. Penn, but the statue, not surprisingly, didn't move. "Guess he didn't see us."

"Guess not," Joy agreed. "He's probably too busy. What do you think he does up there all day? Direct traffic?"

"I should think he wonders where everyone down here is going in such a big hurry. Philadelphia wasn't like this in his day, that's for sure. For one thing, they didn't have an iggull then."

"What's an iggull?" Joy asked, perplexed by the word. She'd never heard it before.

"Come on, I'll show you." He drove north on Broad and found a parking spot in the shadow of the municipal building.

"This is a department store," Joy said as he pulled her into Wanamaker's. "Do they sell 'iggulls' here? Whatever they are. Give me a hint," she coaxed.

He brought her to the center aisle of the store, where there was a large bronze statue. There were benches on either side of it, full of shoppers and more milling around the area. "This is the iggull," he announced.

"Andy, this is an *eagle*," she whispered. "American bald variety."

"To you, maybe, but ask any of these people here what the most famous meeting place in Philadelphia is. They'll tell you it's the iggull. Come on, ask this lady right here." He tugged on her arm and headed for a stout lady who was tapping her foot impatiently and looking extremely cross. "She looks nice and friendly."

Joy giggled and pulled away from him. "Cut it out, Andy." She stepped back and looked up to take in her surroundings. "This isn't a store," she said with awe, "it's a theater, no a grand opera house, for commerce." Tier upon tier of white marble selling floors rose above her. From their balconies shoppers could peer down on the main stage to watch the show. On the second tier there was an enormous gilded pipe organ, the largest she had ever seen. "With musical accompaniment yet," she said, still astonished.

"There are concerts a couple of times a day," Andy remarked. "You've got to hand it to old Mr. Wanamaker." He pointed to the portrait of the founder that faced the eagle. In a contest of wills it was not at all certain who would win; the man was just as fine and fierce as the bird. "It's a brilliant concept—shopping as entertainment."

They strolled around the main floor, enjoying the show—the buttery smells from the bakeshop, the dazzle of the jewelry, the sweet and spicy fragrances from the cosmetics counters. On their way to the door Joy accepted a complimentary spray of cologne from a hostess in a flowered chiffon dress. "'Early Spring' from Sylvana's new collection," the young woman told her, and gave her liberal squirts on both wrists and behind both ears.

They continued down the aisle, and Andy steered her into a deserted vestibule. He brought her close and lifted both of her wrists close to his nose. "Mmmmm," he whispered as he nuzzled her between neck and shoulder. "Smells like things to come."

Between the scent, his nearness and his words, Joy felt enveloped in a hypnotic mist. She leaned against the wall and closed her eyes, letting herself go deeper into this supremely pleasant state. She felt his lips on hers and his strong arms around her. She held on to him and kissed him back. It wasn't too soon now; it was just the right time—but maybe not the right place. She edged away slightly.

"I know," Andy murmured. "If we stay here we're liable to be arrested."

They went back to the car, holding hands and swinging their arms between them. "More tour or shall I feed you?" Andy asked.

"Feed me," she said without hesitation.

They drove back across the Shuylkill River to a French bistro tucked away on a tiny street behind the university. The main room of the restaurant was an enclosed garden, with a great gnarled tree growing up through the roof. At a very private table beside the trunk they ate fluffy spinach omelets, hot raisin muffins and drank glasses of fruity Beaujolais. A small string quartet tucked away in the far corner of the room played Vivaldi, Mozart and Haydn. They sat for a long time over coffee, enjoying the place, the music, being together.

"I feel I've known you for a long time," Andy said as they walked back to the car. "It's hard to believe it's been just over a week."

"For me, too," Joy allowed. "It feels like a whole new life to me. I can't imagine what I did with my time back in New York. My days are so full here. And everything I do is connected." *To you, through you*, she wanted to add.

"This week has meant a lot to me too, Joy. Having you at the theater has filled a gap that I've tried to pretend didn't exist for a long time." He took her hand and pulled back the cuff of her mitten to kiss it. "I'm so glad you've come into my life, sunshine."

Her cheeks flamed at his words; the cold drops that fell on them melted instantly. She glanced up at the gray clouds. "Better make that snowflake," she said, and pressed his cold hand to her face.

At the top of his lungs, Andy began to sing, "You are my snowflake, my only—"

To an amused passerby, Joy said, "I don't know this lunatic, never saw him before in my life." She started to walk away from him; he followed, still singing. She quickened her pace, and he kept up; she skipped, then ran, and soon they were racing down the street, laughing and panting. He caught up with her as they reached the car and pinned her against it.

"You won't melt away on me, will you, snowflake?"

"If you keep looking at me like that I will," she said in a raw whisper.

He put his arms around her and held her close to his chest. "Warmest snowflake I ever held," he said with a soft laugh.

"Not to mention the biggest," she countered.

He drew back and looked at her. "Come to think of it you don't have six points and a crystalline structure."

"Not the last time I looked."

Arms around each other's waist, they walked around the car to the passenger side, and Andy unlocked the door and opened it for her. "How about some after-lunch culture?" he suggested.

As they rounded Logan Circle a few minutes later and continued up the Benjamin Franklin Parkway, Joy began to have the feeling she'd been there before, although she knew she never had. "I don't know why, but this looks familiar," she said.

"Ever see the movie *Rocky*?"

"Of course," she realized. She raised both arms above her head—as far as she was able in the car—and waved them. "Da-da-dee-e-e-e, da-da-daa-a-a," she sang the *Rocky* theme. "Those are the steps Rocky ran up during his training runs." Unlike the scenes in the movie, the museum itself dwarfed the steps. It was an imposing replica of a Greek temple with portico, triangular frieze and papyrus-capped columns, cast in a stone with unusual orange-pink undertones. "Better him than me," she said, looking once again at the long flight of steps.

"Or me," Andy said. "I can't see knocking yourself out to let some other guy punch you in the snout."

"*Rocky*'s not about fighting so much as slugging it out with life. You ought to know that. You're a Rocky. Everyone said you couldn't get the theater to go the distance, but you have. And think of all the other great fighting plays and movies—*Golden Boy*, *Requiem for a Heavyweight, Somebody Up There Likes Me*. They're all metaphors for staying in the ring, even when life puts you up against the ropes."

"I get the metaphor. It's fighting itself I don't get. I can see hauling off and hitting somebody in the heat of the moment, but not preparing for it, doing it for an audience."

"Ever been to a professional fight?"

"I suppose you have," he said skeptically.

"Only once, when I was working on a scene from *Golden Boy* for an acting class. My partner and I went. It's not just bloodthirsty and violent. There's real skill and stamina involved and—"

"Tell that to all the guys with brain damage. And all the guys who fix fights."

"I didn't say there aren't any problems with boxing, but I can understand why people are drawn to it, why they do it. Just because you don't like something or believe in it doesn't necessarily mean other people can't or shouldn't."

"Anything goes, right? Everyone should live by their own standards." He pulled the car into a parking lot behind the museum. "That would put us in a nice muddle."

"No, anything doesn't go. But it would be a lot easier to agree on common standards if some people weren't so self-righteous about theirs."

"Meaning me?" he asked belligerently.

"I think we're having our first fight," Joy said quietly.

"Our first heated discussion," he answered after a moment with a grudging smile.

"We can't agree on everything."

"No. I guess not."

They entered the museum, and Andy led her up a flight of stairs and around to the front of the building. They stopped outside to enjoy the view from the portico, a straight line to city hall. The snow was coming down harder now, but the statue of William Penn stood out clearly, dull green against the white sky. Because of the distance and the position of the museum atop a hill, it seemed as if they were on the same level as the statue. If there had been a highway in the air, they could have walked right up and stood beside him.

Joy raised her arm and waved vigorously to Penn. "I guess he's still too busy to wave back," she said in an attempt to restore the light mood. But Andy only smiled thinly and continued staring pensively at the cityscape below them.

"Are we okay?" he asked finally. She wasn't the first person to have pointed out his tendency to be rigid, unbending. He'd lost the only woman he ever cared about—before Joy—because of it. He didn't want to make the same mistake again.

"Of course," she assured him, linking her arm through his. "It was nothing." She hadn't seen him moody or inward before. Maybe she'd hit a pet peeve with the subject of boxing.

"No," he said. "It was something. I'm sorry if I got bent out of shape."

"And I'm sorry if I rubbed you the wrong way."

"Oh, I don't know if you could rub me the wrong way." He grabbed her hand and moved it first over his snow-damp hair, one way and then the other, then back and forth over his face. "See?" he asked with a grin.

Joy pulled her hand away and put her palm over his nose, rubbing the tip in a circle. "Not even like this?"

"Hey, cut it out," he said with a muffled, nasal laugh, and pushed her hand away. "That tickles." He chucked her under the chin and then shook the light film of snow from the strands of hair that peeked out from under her cap. "Let's go back in before we turn into snow people."

She brushed the flakes from his hair and shoulders, and they left the portico hand in hand. Andy steered them to the American wing and to a small room crammed with paintings by Thomas Eakins, one of Philadelphia's most famous artists. There were several of his signature paintings of sculling on the Schuylkill, but his insightful portraits interested them more than the rowing scenes.

They spent a long time in front of *The Actress*, a dark brooding study of a not so young woman half-collapsed in a large carved wooden chair, gripping its arms with tense, beautiful hands. The background, done in browns and a sickly green, was reflected in the pallor of the actress's face. The only spot of bright color was the woman's dress, a pink-red that might have been garish on a happier, less refined subject. On the floor beside the chair, as if they had dropped from her hands, were a script and a check.

Talking in low, private whispers, Joy and Andy sat on a bench in front of the painting and made up stories about the actress—what she was doing in the room, why she was so pale, what script she was reading, the meaning of the check.

"You ought to commission someone to write a play about her, inspired by her," she suggested.

"What a terrific idea!" he exclaimed so loudly that he drew a few annoyed glances from other patrons. He lowered his voice. "It would be great for the theater.

Maybe we could tie it in with an Eakins celebration. Make it a city-wide event."

He was so animated she could almost hear his brain clicking as he spoke. "Hold on there. You haven't got the play yet."

"No, but we've got the idea, the spark. The rest will follow from that." He got to his feet. "Would you mind not seeing anything else today? I want to keep her image strong in my mind, not dilute it with any others."

"We can come back another day," she said. Already he was edging away from the bench. *He's like a horse in the starting gate*, she thought, *anxious for the race to begin.*

"How about one more stop and then we'll go home and light a fire?" he suggested as they walked briskly to the car. He unlocked and opened the door for her. "Maybe more than one fire," he whispered as she folded herself inside.

His words sent another of the increasingly familiar tremors shaking through her. What was a little tiff, she asked herself as she reached across to unlock his door, when they agreed on important things, like good ideas for plays. The thought produced an expansive pride that mingled nicely with her other heightened senses.

"For the past couple of years," Andy said as he pulled out of the parking lot, "I've been rooting around for an idea that would tie the theater in more closely with the city and its past and present. So many of our regional distinctions are being lost these days. Everywhere you go you find the same national chains, national brands. Jackson, Mississippi, isn't so different from Jackson Hole, Wyoming. Regional theaters can help preserve an area's particular characteristics. I've wanted to do more of that at the Arc and now I see how I can. How *we* can," he amended, and continued his monologue. "This past week has been so exciting for me—watching you grow in rehearsals, seeing you gain confidence and take on responsibilities in the office as well. It's been a relief, too. Gretchen is worth her weight in gold where details are concerned, but I need to have someone working with me whose artistic judgment I can rely on. I've been doing this alone a long time, Joy. I think we'd make a great team."

"What are you asking of me?" she asked, feeling a bit like Alice being beckoned down the rabbit hole.

"To consider sticking around after the show is over."

"Andy, that's almost two months down the line. How can you be sure you'll want me to stay?"

"I know what I want, Joy, and I go after it. I told you that before."

"So you did," she said thoughtfully. *But you also told me that I don't make clear choices, that I let myself be swept away by whatever currents I encounter. And you, Andy Thornhill, are an extremely strong current.* "I'll think about it," she told him cautiously.

The note of uncertainty was not lost on Andy, and he had to remind himself not to push her or press her. She said she'd think about it; now he had to give her room to do so. "You're in for a real treat tonight. Chicken à la Andy. We have to stop and get the ingredients, though."

They returned to Center City, and Andy parked the car across the street from a large reddish stone building. "The Reading Terminal Market," he announced.

"I hope that means it's at the end of a line and not what happens to you after you eat the food."

Andy groaned and gave her a wry smile. "You'll eat those words," he promised. "This used to be the station for the main commuter railway. A new one's been built, but the market was preserved."

After her first minute in the marvelous market, Joy wanted to eat more than words. The smells alone were enough to make her salivate.

"The first thing I always do," Andy said, "is get a hot pretzel. If I didn't I'd be tempted to buy one of everything in sight." He stepped up to a stand and bought two fat freshly baked soft pretzels, liberally buttered and lightly salted. Behind the open counter a young Amish woman rolled and twisted dough with deft, practiced strokes.

"I didn't know how good these could be," she told Andy as they strolled down the aisle. "They sure beat those heavy doughy things the hot dog vendors sell in New York."

"Another reason for sticking around," he said, sounding smug even to his own ears. "Come on," he covered quickly. "Let's go find us a nice plump chicken. I've got a favorite Lancaster County butcher. Over this way."

Many Amish came to the market every day with freshly killed poultry, sausages, scrapple and cold cuts, cheeses, baked goods, jams and jellies, honey, herbs and handicrafts. About a third of the stands were staffed by men with long hair and beards, wearing rimless glasses, plain shirts and black trousers with suspenders. The women by their sides wore simple cotton dresses and dark stockings and pulled their hair into buns covered with transparent starched white caps. Joy was taken aback when she noticed one of the younger women wearing a pair of gray running shoes with the logo of a fashionable manufacturer. She nudged Andy and pointed discreetly. They smiled together at the incongruous sight. "Practical, though, if you're going to be on your feet all day," she commented.

With the discerning eye of a scrupulous housewife, Andy selected a chicken and asked for it to be cut into serving pieces. He also purchased a pound of hand-cut egg noodles, butter, free-range eggs and breakfast sausages. They drooled at the bakery counters and finally selected an apple strudel and a loaf of whole grain bread. After the surliness in most New York shops, Joy appreciated the cheerful politeness with which they were served. But she didn't say anything about it to Andy; it might occasion another of his cutting comments about the city she had chosen to live in. Well, she thought philosophically, at least she didn't have to guess at what he was thinking. Too many of the men she'd dated were closemouthed and secretive. Andy's directness was a pleasant change.

They continued around the market, stopping to listen to a dulcimer player, to watch a man shucking clams and oysters, to sniff the rounds of provolone and garlicky salamis hanging above an Italian food purveyor. Their final stop was the greengrocer, where Andy loaded up on onions, mushrooms and broccoli.

Outside the snow was falling more heavily and starting to stick to the pavements, which were becoming slick underfoot. Traffic was moving slowly and carefully, and Andy put on the car radio for a forecast. It was supposed to snow all night, with accumulations of a foot or more. "We might be snowed in together," he ventured.

"I can think of worse fates," Joy said softly.

"Far worse," Andy agreed.

Back at the Arc they scampered through the snow to the carriage house and went through to Andy's quarters. He brought in an extra load of wood from the pile out back and closed off the French doors to the office. "I don't want anyone barging in accidentally," he said as he turned the key in the lock. "People have a habit of forgetting my occasional days off."

Joy unloaded the groceries while Andy lit a fire. When it was roaring, he opened a chilled bottle of Beaujolais Nouveau, and they lounged in front of the fire on a pile of plump cushions. The last of the day's light faded, and with it the pace of the day slowed to a languid nighttime rhythm.

They let the leaps and crackles of the fire entertain them, talking only occasionally, snatches of conversation that sparked and burned down like the fire when fueled by a new log or a gust of wind. Later Joy sat on a stool and watched the preparation of chicken à la Andy, a fricassee with onions and mushrooms, white wine and herbs. The chef let her supervise the boiling and buttering of the noodles and the steaming of the broccoli while he put the finishing touches on the chicken. They emptied the wine bottle with dinner and somehow managed to find room for tiny slivers of the strudel with cinnamon-scented coffee.

"My compliments to the chef," Joy said when they were curled up on the sofa sipping snifters of brandy.

"Compliments? Is that all the chef gets? Compliments?"

"What else could a chef want besides compliments and clean plates? Both of which you've had," she pointed out.

"He might want an after-dinner kiss," he suggested, removing the snifter from her hand.

"Is that like an after-dinner mint?" she murmured as his arms circled her waist.

"Better. And what comes after the kiss will be even better. I need you, Joy. I want you."

The day, all the days since she'd met him, had been building inexorably to this moment. Now that it had arrived she had a brief irrational desire to postpone it, to continue their days forever, despite the delights the beckoning night and his beckoning arms promised.

Into her momentary confusion came Juliet's words, the words she had spoken as she waited for Romeo to come to her chamber so they might consummate their secret marriage. Joy began to recite them in a taut, hushed voice. "'Come night, come Romeo, come thou day in night; for thou wilt lie upon the wings of night, whiter than new snow upon a raven's back.'"

She's perfect, he thought, *absolutely and utterly perfect*. "The rest," he said urgently. "Do you remember the rest?"

The words came to her easily, for they belonged as much to this moment as to the one the Bard had created. "'Come gentle night, come loving black-browed night, give me my Romeo, and when he shall die, take him and cut him out in little stars and he shall make the face of heaven so fine, that all the world will be in love with night, and pay no worship to the garish sun.'"

Once she had said the piece there was no returning to day. She tumbled willingly into the arms that pulled her close, willingly kissed the mouth that sent ripples of icy tingles rolling through her. The night was theirs; they would claim it together.

She wrapped her arms around him, and he lowered her gently against the arm of the sofa. His kiss had many currents, and she let them waft her where they would—up, down, over and back into a feeling of pure freedom, curiously charged and relaxed at the same time.

His left hand cradled her head and his right caressed her face, her neck, the length of her body, then sneaked under her sweater to unhook her bra and fondle a breast. He rolled the nipple against the palm of his hand, and a small sigh escaped her lips. The icy ripples he had started with his kiss turned to fiery waves of pleasure.

"I've never wanted anyone the way I want you, Joy. I have such feelings for you. Such strong feelings," he repeated, and buried his face in her neck. "I've wanted to make love with you almost from the first moment I saw you. Now, after all I've seen of you, learned of you, I *need* to make love to you, need it as I need to breathe. It's the only way I can show you how I feel."

She went limp in his arms; she had dreamed so long of passion like this that she had begun to believe it existed only in her imagination. But here it was; she was living her dreams with Andy. Not only living them, but building vibrant, powerful new ones every moment they were together.

He lifted her deftly from the couch and set her down on the cushions in front of the crackling fire. He knelt beside her and helped her out of her clothes, then shed his hastily.

"You're gorgeous," he said, drinking in every inch of her nude body with his eyes. Her nipples hardened from his mere glance, and when he reached out to graze her breast a tremor coursed through her.

Her sense of time disintegrated; for minutes, hours, weeks he suckled at her breasts, tenderly laving each rigid nipple with his tongue. Her sense of space collapsed when his lips moved down to her belly, her thighs, the throbbing wanting needing place between her legs. She held on to his shoulders and arched to meet his exquisite caresses. Just short of total ecstasy he stopped, positioned himself above her and with tantalizing slowness slipped into her warm waiting wetness.

Propped on his arms, he circled inside her languidly and gazed into her eyes. Looking up at him, she felt she could see past his eyes, past his face, all the way to his heart. "Andy," she whispered.

"What is it, my joy?"

"I just wanted to say your name."

"Say it again for me."

"Andy," she breathed once more.

Neither of them wanted or needed to hurry. They had the rest of the night to be together. They kissed and caressed each other's body, exploring, experimenting, stoking the fires that burned within, until they were both red-hot with a desire that demanded quenching. The waves of cool delicious ecstasy that washed over them at the end had them clinging to each other like two shipwrecked sailors. Only when they began to shiver did they realize the fire beside them had died; only a few glowing embers remained.

Andy reached up and pulled an afghan from the back of the sofa. He laid it over them, and Joy settled her head on his shoulder. He pushed aside the damp strands of hair from her forehead and planted a soft kiss there. "Didn't I tell you we'd make a great team?" he asked happily.

"Care to try for a doubleheader?" she asked, and snuggled against him suggestively. Their lovemaking had surpassed any expectations she'd ever had. Even though she was sated, she couldn't suppress the joyful thought of future sessions.

"Not right now, not even with you, my little witch. But check with me again later," he said with a broad grin.

"I'll do that," she murmured.

Later, wrapped together in the afghan, they climbed the stairs to the loft and slept curled in each other's arms on Andy's low platform bed. It was close to dawn when they reached for each other again. When they finally got up the next morning, they found it had snowed all night, and the world was covered with a blanket of snow as fresh and pure as the feelings they had discovered in each other.

7

THE NEXT THREE WEEKS were like a continuous spin in an amusement park ride Joy had once been on. It whirled so fast that centrifugal force pinned her to the wall of the twirling cylinder, even when the floor was lowered from beneath her feet. She became welded to the Arc by her passion for theater itself and by her increasingly deep feelings for Andy.

Besides rehearsing she took on many other duties. She and Andy hit upon the idea of sponsoring a contest for a play inspired by Eakins's *The Actress*, and she took on the task of setting up the rules, finding funding and publicizing it. She plowed through the long-neglected stack of submissions and found a gem that Andy was seriously considering for the coming season.

She spent more and more time at the carriage house with Andy, often staying overnight, using her room at the parish house when she needed quiet time to work on her role or to think. She attended communal lunches infrequently and usually dashed in at midday for something to take back to the office for the two of them. "I thought maybe you would get our Mr. Whirligig in here for a proper meal now and then," Mrs. C often chided her, "but you're just like him. Go on, go on," she would cluck in a wounded tone, at the same time pressing a napkinful of oatmeal cookies or a pair of sweet juicy oranges into Joy's hands.

Andy's hard work at courting critics paid off, and he won commitments from both New York and national news media reviewers to attend the opening performance of *Sisters and Daughters*. Feeling expansive and confident, he decided to turn the usual opening night party for cast and a few friends and family into a gala event; Joy, with the help of the student intern Janet Lawton, supervised the sending of invitations, the caterer and the myriad details of a successful party.

They both worked tirelessly from morning to night, and when they could do no more they tumbled eagerly into each other's arms, one passion fueling the other, firing a white-hot heat that radiated between them.

It had a cooling effect on others, though. The few times she and Andy sat down to lunch with everybody there were digs, good-natured on the surface, but not without bite. "Oh, is that you, Andy?" from Sarah. "I hardly recognized you. You've been only a voice in the dark for so long. Didn't you used to have a beard?" And a deadpan zinger from Mark, "If I'd known that royalty were joining us for luncheon, I'd have worn a tie and jacket. No shirt, of course, just the tie and jacket."

Joy and Andy took the ribbing graciously—and gave back as good as they got. They knew they'd set themselves off from the group, but not out of malice or snobbery, only out of a need to be with each other, to learn everything they could about each other in the shortest possible time. Gretchen was the only one who didn't join in the general razzing; she did her usual efficient job and kept her own counsel. Though she never said a spiteful word or behaved unpleasantly, once or twice Joy caught Gretchen staring at her with a thoughtful, determined look that made her uncomfortable. It was the only tiny blot on an otherwise idyllic time.

There was the usual last-minute hysteria in the days before opening—the cast stumbling over changes in the script, unable to recall which of the feverish revisions were the latest; a set piece that collapsed in the middle of a tense scene; a desk drawer that jammed at a crucial moment; costumes that were too long, too short, too baggy, too tight. Everyone wore their nerves in a different style—cutting sarcasm from Mark; stoic manliness from Ken; taut silence from Lila; backhanded sniping from Sarah; lightning bolts of anger from Harvey. Andy became positively military, barking out stiff commands in moments of crisis.

Joy broke her usual pattern of barely controlled panic and became weepy. Everything from the morning weather report to a cross word or look was a provocation to tears. She wasn't sure what had occasioned the unusual state. Perhaps all the strong emotions in the air had brought it on—her heart-tugging feelings for Andy, her growing love for the Arc itself, building what she knew to be the strongest performance of her career in one of the best new plays she had seen or read in years. She kept the tears bravely at bay while relearning a scene for the fifth time, through the costume fittings and the interminable technical rehearsal where lighting and sound cues were set and reset, and scene changes practiced until all the technical aspects of the show were running smoothly. By the time they had completed the dress rehearsal, she felt as if her head were swimming in hot saltwater. In midsentence, while relaxing with Andy after the rehearsal, she broke down.

"I can't do it. I can't go on," she sobbed.

He put an arm around her tenderly. "None of us can. But we will," he soothed to no avail. Her shoulders continued to heave and shake, and the tears streamed down her cheeks. "You're getting your tea all salty," he said finally.

She giggled through her tears and looked down. A large drop plopped loudly into her mug. "You're right," she sniffled, and he took the tea from her and offered a paper napkin to mop her face.

"Feel better?"

She heaved a loud sigh and assessed herself. "Yeah. I needed that."

Neither of them slept much that night; they lay quietly in wait for day, holding hands, dozing now and then. At first light Joy could no longer lie still. She pulled on tights and leotard and did her morning workout, then shared a silent breakfast with Andy.

There was little for Joy to do that day; Andy had called the cast for a brief meeting in the morning, to give notes and a pep talk, and go over last minute technical details. In the afternoon she took care of a few things for the party, went out for some fresh air and a walk and then retreated to her own room to center herself for the evening's performance.

She arrived at the women's dressing room well before the half hour call and found it empty. She hung her party dress on the rack, stripped off her clothes and changed into the comfortable terry cloth robe that was her usual dressing room attire. She had just sat down to brush back her hair and start on her makeup when Sarah and Lila arrived. Hard on their heels was Gretchen with a large package wrapped in florist's paper.

Harlequin Temptation Free Gifts–Free Prizes 98786

YES I'll try the Harlequin Preview Service under the terms specified herein. Send me 4 free books and all the other FREE GIFTS. I understand that I also automatically qualify for ALL "Super Celebration" prizes and prize features advertised in 1986. I have written my birthday below. Tell me on my birthday what I win.

WIN A GREAT PRIZE

◀ If you are NOT signing up for Preview Service, DO NOT use seal. You can win anyway.

FILL IN BIRTHDAY INFORMATION BELOW

MONTH | DATE

this month's featured prize—a dozen roses + 12 $100 bills on winner's birthday + as an added bonus lovely 14k birthstone earrings for 101 other winners.

PLEASE PRINT

142 CIX 2513

NAME

ADDRESS   APT #

CITY

STATE   ZIP

Gift offer limited to new subscribers, one per household, and terms and prices subject to change.

Harlequin
"Super Celebration" Sweepstakes

901 Fuhrmann Blvd.
P.O. Box 1867
Buffalo, NY 14240-1867

PLACE
1ST CLASS
STAMP
HERE

"I'm surprised Andy remembered me and Lila," Sarah said as she looked at the card stapled to the top of the package.

"How do you know they're from Andy?" Joy asked.

"He always sends flowers on opening night," Lila replied. "Cigars to the men's dressing room."

"Mind if I go ahead?" Sarah asked, already starting to rip the paper.

"Go right ahead," Lila and Joy said in unison, deferring to Sarah's impatience.

The older woman uncovered a beautiful arrangement of red and white carnations and cheerful white pompons. Picking up the card, she read it aloud. "Thanks for all your terrific work. I know we'll have a great run. Break a leg, signed Andy." Turning to Joy, she said, "Sorry, no personal message for you. But I suppose you've already had yours." She added a lusty chuckle.

Joy had no polite answer for Sarah, so she smiled enigmatically and returned to pinning up her hair. She was glad Andy had not singled her out, either on the card or with separate flowers. She got a warm rush in her stomach thinking about his concern and regard for the cast. And for her. She'd seen him only in passing that afternoon, but he'd taken her aside for a private moment, kissed her, told her she'd put together a marvelous performance and wished her *merde.* She wished him the same—it was bad luck to wish anyone connected with a show good luck before a performance.

Gretchen returned to announce the half hour. The three women looked at one another and fell silent. The half hour call on opening night hit every performer sharply. It marked the end of preparation and underscored the imminence of facing the audience to ask for their understanding and approval of four weeks of hard work. There was nothing to do now but finish dressing and face the music.

Fifteen quiet minutes passed, and Gretchen knocked and announced the quarter hour, then five minutes, then the final summons, "First act beginners, please." Joy stood, smoothed her skirt, wriggled her numb toes, shook her hands and with a nod to Sarah and Lila followed Gretchen into the wings. The weepy feeling returned and threatened to engulf her. Her hands grew icy, and she trembled involuntarily. She saw the houselights dim and disappear. Then the stage went to black, and she forced one foot in front of the other toward her opening pose on the sofa. The play was beginning.

THE NEXT THING Joy really heard was the vigorous applause at the final blackout. The reception grew as the company assembled onstage for a group bow. Then each individual stepped forward to accept the appreciation of the crowd. Joy curtsied deeply when her turn came and looked up with surprise when she heard first one and then another shout of "Brava" coming from the house. She smiled gratefully and bowed her head in acknowledgment, thrilled to the core. It was the first time she had received that very special sign of approval.

The company took two more group bows, and then Andy and Gerry Westover joined them onstage for another round of applause. Andy stepped halfway into the wings to retrieve the bouquet of roses he had ordered for Gerry and presented them to her. The audience clapped loudly at the gesture and demanded solo bows from both the author and director. After a final ensemble bow, the eight staggered into the wings, where they applauded Gretchen and her crew for all their hard work behind the scenes.

Andy managed to whisper a quick, "You were fabulous," and pass his hand lovingly across her bottom before disappearing to attend to his duties as host. She stayed with the cast and crew for a moment and then broke away to the dressing room. Not until she had removed and hung up her costume did she begin to comprehend the enormity of the evening, the success of the play, her performance in it, Andy's direction of it. *If only the reviews are as good as the audience reaction*, she wished happily as she creamed off her makeup. A sense of lightness, of floating an inch or two above the ground, began to overtake her as she brushed her hair out of Barbara's severe style and into her own natural flowing waves. She changed out of Barbara's practical underclothes into wispy red lace panties and camisole and stepped into her party dress—red crepe shot with gold threads in a flapper style with V-neck, dropped waist and accordion-pleated skirt—and buckled her shapely feet into high-heeled red sandals.

She was the first cast member to arrive at the parish house for the party and was nearly bowled over by the reception she received. People rushed up to shake her hand and offer praise. She had been complimented on performances before but never so effusively or lavishly. Before she'd even taken a glass of wine from a passing waiter she started to feel high.

Finally she was able to make her way into the dining room to find Janet and make sure everything was going well with the food and drink. She found her by the kitchen door, asking the caterer to get one of the waiters to circulate with a tray of soft drinks for those who did not care for wine. "Everything under control?" she asked.

Janet nodded and pointed to the table, which was laden with trays of cheeses, baskets of bread and crackers, copper chafing dishes filled with hot hors d'oeuvres and a colorful centerpiece of crudités and dips. "It looks beautiful, doesn't it? You made a good choice with the caterer. She really knows what she's doing."

The mouth-watering array of food made Joy realize she hadn't eaten since fixing herself a small snack late in the afternoon. "The food looks too good to resist," she said to Janet, and took one of the small plates from the stack on the corner of the table and began to pile it with a sampling of the fare. But before she'd downed her first hot spinach ball, she was approached by a man she recognized with a start as one of the *New York Times*'s most caustic reviewers. He introduced himself, but said nothing about the play or her performance. *Saving it all for print*, she thought.

"I've seen you somewhere before, haven't I?" the critic asked.

"*Pie in the Sky*," Joy suggested, hoping she wouldn't have to reveal it as her only New York credit other than the frequent showcases and workshops she had participated in.

"Yes, of course," he said.

They chatted amiably for a few minutes, Joy very much aware that the reviewer was sizing her up and annoyed at her self-consciousness. Finally someone else buttonholed him, and she took a plateful of hors d'oeuvres and moved away to circulate.

After the encounter with the reviewer, Joy had a wonderful time matching faces to the names she knew so well from the invitation list. Andy presented her to his parents, his brothers and their wives. All three sons took strongly after their father in looks, but of the three only Andy had not adopted the elder Thornhill's controlled conservative demeanor. All four were dressed in tuxedos, but Andy wore his with a dashing red velvet tie that would have looked out of place on the others.

By two o'clock only the cast members, the author and the designers, some with friends or families, were still around, and Joy told the caterer she could start to clear up. Suddenly drained of energy, she flopped down in one of the armchairs. She hadn't noticed it until she sat down, but her calves were aching from standing for hours in such high heels. She loosened the straps of her sandals and propped her feet up on the coffee table.

Andy called for attention and conversations tapered off. "I want to thank all of you for your contributions—individual and collective—to tonight's success. I don't know when I've been as excited about a play or a production. The Arc has turned a corner tonight, moved into a new era of expansion, greater visibility, greater impact, and I'm proud of all of—"

"Don't you want to wait for the reviews before saying all this mushy stuff?" Mark cut in.

"I've got a hunch they'll be quite good," Andy said with a laugh, "but even if they're not, the flowery speech still stands. But enough of waxing eloquent. The call is at seven tomorrow for notes, people. You were good—but not perfect," he added to a chorus of groans and hisses. "Go home now, get some rest and let's see if we can put on an even better show tomorrow."

The group slowly filtered out or up to their rooms, and Andy and Joy started for the carriage house, arms around each other's waist, savoring the last moments of a long momentous night. They climbed to the sleeping loft, undressed quickly and snuggled close under the covers.

"Do you know how good you were tonight?" he asked softly.

"I'm not sure," she said. "I keep waiting for someone to wake me up."

"I could hardly take notes during your scenes." He put his hand under her chin and lifted her face. "You're very special, Joy. My joy."

"Oh, Andy," she breathed, hardly able to bear the intensity of his gaze, the force of the naked need she saw there. He asked so much of her, and she was afraid she couldn't satisfy him, couldn't give him every ounce of herself as he demanded.

His mouth moved over hers, and she closed her eyes, willing to give him what she could, hoping it would be enough. He took her offering readily, and she relaxed into his caress. With a kiss or two more her fears faded, and she climbed aboard the magic carpet of passion he had spread before them. Together they flew off on a long ecstatic journey that continued throughout the night and well into the dawn.

8

"WHAT ARE YOU LOOKING so smug about?" Joy said to Andy over tea on Friday afternoon. He'd been looking like this since lunchtime, and she was itching to know why. "Still gloating over the reviews?"

"If anyone should be gloating, it's you." The production's notices had been enthusiastic, and Joy's personal mentions especially so.

"I'm too thrilled to gloat. Come on, give, what's up?"

"I don't know what you're talking about."

"Ha! If you were a cat, Andy Thornhill, your whiskers would be dripping sweet cream right now."

"Perhaps they would, my dear." He dazzled her with a self-satisfied smile.

"Won't you give me a hint?" she coaxed, snuggling up close and kissing him on the cheek.

He pushed her away playfully. "That will get you nowhere," he stated firmly.

"All right," she said, more intrigued than ever, "if you won't tell me, I shall deprive you of my company." It was almost six, and she needed time to shift gears before the performance. Now that there were no rehearsals, she was spending all day in the office, freeing Andy and Gretchen to concentrate on preparations for rehearsals for the next production, which were to begin on Monday.

"Which you would have done in five or ten minutes, anyway," he pointed out.

"You can be quite exasperating at times." She drained her mug and got up. "If you're very lucky, you'll see me later."

"And if *you're* very lucky, I might buy you a cheese steak after the show."

"Hmph! The last of the big spenders." She kissed him lightly on the forehead and went off to her room.

Andy took a long time to join the cast for notes after the performance that night. He apologized for keeping everyone waiting. "But I don't think you're going to mind when you hear what I have to say. Last night a representative of the Phillips Organization saw the show." A ripple of excitement passed through the room—Joshua Phillips was one of Broadway's most powerful producers. "He liked what he saw and recommended that Phillips himself come down tonight. There's trouble with the union about a play they were bringing over from England and they're looking for a replacement. I didn't tell any of you—" he looked significantly at Joy "—because I didn't want you to be nervous about it. You gave a good performance tonight, people—" he paused for a long beat "—and I'm going to New York tomorrow to talk to Phillips about a Broadway option."

There was stunned silence for a moment and then a spontaneous cheer resounded through the room. Joy whooped and applauded with the others, but hardly heard the noise for the ringing that filled her head. She felt as if she'd been standing in a bell tower for hours and was deaf to anything but wildly pealing bells. Every actor who performed in regional theater joked about riding back into town on a Broadway option; the limousine might not be hers yet, but it was parked at the curb.

"Okay, okay, settle down, people. You were good tonight, but there's still room for improvement." Andy waggled his clipboard at them. "Notes, people. Listen up." When he got to the end of the list, he asked for questions.

Ken spoke up. "About the Phillips Organization, Andy, will you be discussing an option on the play or the production?"

"The production," he answered without hesitation. "As far as I'm concerned, all of you are this play as much as the words Gerry put on paper. But you have to remember that although the Arc currently holds the rights to the play, Gerry has the ultimate say in what happens to her work. Anyone else?"

Heads shook soberly. *It's like* The Wizard of Oz, Joy thought. *The yellow brick road is paved with obstacles.* But unlike Dorothy neither she nor anyone else at the Arc owned a magic pair of ruby-red slippers.

Later, as they were munching steak sandwiches in his car in front of Anthony's, Andy asked Joy, "Do you want to come up to the city with me tomorrow?"

"It would be fun, but I don't want to tire myself out for the performance," she said with regret. Busy as she was she'd been missing New York, its variety, its insistence, its demands.

"I understand. I thought I could use the moral support, though. Josh Phillips is a tough nut to crack."

"You're no bowl of rice pudding."

"Oh, I don't know. I quiver sometimes—when I see you, when I'm with you." He stroked her cheek, her hair. "And speaking of dessert..." He kissed her firmly, hungrily. "Could I convince you to move on to the next course?"

"I think that could be arranged," she answered, nibbling seductively on his bottom lip.

JOSH PHILLIPS PROVED TO BE not only tough but intractable. He didn't want the production at all; he wanted the play to produce his own way, with name players. He offered Andy the chance to direct, but wouldn't take the risk of an unknown playwright and a director with no New York credits without backing them up with star actors, a choice he would control. "I'm not in this business to lose money," he told Andy bluntly.

Andy tried every tactic he could think of, but couldn't get Phillips to budge from his position. By the end of the meeting only two things were certain—the production would not move intact from Philadelphia to Broadway, and Andy's fury.

He left the office and raced back to the car, eager to leave New York far behind him. He welcomed the seedy bleakness of the Lincoln Tunnel and the first ugly stretch of the New Jersey Turnpike. They matched his mood exactly. The day had intensified his opinions about theater in New York—money dictated the decisions. Everything else—creativity, aesthetics, truth, vision, all the things that the theater was about for him—came after, far after. He'd been right to steer clear of New York, and he would continue to stay away.

He had to admit, though, that he had been as excited as the rest of the cast and Gerry Westover about the possibility of taking the show to New York. It would have moved the Arc farther into the mainstream, made it a force to be reckoned with. And he would have welcomed the personal triumph, too. He couldn't deny that. But there was no question of his directing if he couldn't bring the whole production with him; he would never consider being involved with a show where he didn't have the final say about who was in the cast.

So much for New York, he thought with a snort. Well, to hell with it. He and Joy would stay in Philadelphia and build a real, substantial life there. They didn't need tinsel or glitter or glitz to be happy together, to do good solid work. The past month had proved that.

It had been the best month of his life. For once everything meshed, everything important, that is— work and love. With Brenda there had been a constant wrangle about time. The time he spent at the theater, the time he wasn't spending with her. But Joy's life was the theater, just as his was. They could be together virtually every minute of the day and night and miss neither work nor love. It was easy to imagine going on this way with her forever.

Forever. That could mean only one thing. He loved her; he'd known that from the moment she'd spontaneously recited Juliet's speech before they'd made love for the first time. His feelings hadn't changed since then; they had only grown deeper and stronger. He would ask her to marry him. It was the right thing to do, the only thing to do, the logical, natural outcome of their time together. He was certain of it. "I'm going to ask her to marry me," he said aloud with a mixture of wonder, awe and excitement.

The minute he said the words the tightness in his chest began to loosen. He began to laugh at himself. How could he have missed such an obvious solution?

Ever since the show opened he'd been wondering how to keep Joy with him at the Arc. There was no part for her in the next production, and he'd hoped she'd stay on as assistant producer. Now he knew. He loved her; he'd known that for weeks. Happily, elatedly, he began to plan their future—complete with babies and a pet collie.

The fantasy carried him merrily down the highway, and only when he crossed the Walt Whitman Bridge did he start thinking of breaking the news about his meeting with Phillips to Gerry and the cast. He'd start with Gerry, going directly to her apartment to avoid arriving at the theater until curtain time. Better to have the actors antsy before the performance than depressed, he decided.

JOY SPENT THE MORNING taking care of practical things—her nails, her hair, the laundry. She tried to read at the Laundromat, but her eyes kept straying from the page as she became lost in thought. During rehearsals it had seemed that she had a long time left in Philadelphia; now that the show was up and running the time seemed very short.

She was of two minds about going back to New York. She would miss the cozy self-contained world of the Arc, and she would miss Andy desperately. On the other hand, with all she'd learned as an actress and about herself, she was sure she could handle New York with much more confidence and assurance. She would find a new agent and start to work steadily; her dreams would finally begin to come true. She longed to give it a try, but felt an almost equal reluctance to leave the relative security of the Arc—and Andy.

Andy. She had grown so close to him in so short a time. Just the thought of him made her insides tumble faster than the clothes in the dryer in front of her. She was happier, more content with him than she could have imagined; their lives touched in so many ways. But he had that stubborn streak, that I'm-right-the-world's-wrong attitude that sometimes surfaced. She admired his strong convictions, but wished he didn't get so heated up when everybody else didn't share them.

Going to New York with the Arc company would be the best of all possible worlds. She wouldn't have to separate from Andy or the security of the company, but she'd also be performing on Broadway. That had been her dream ever since her tenth birthday when she'd seen her first Broadway show. It was like a separate living thing; she had fed it, had nurtured it, had loved it. In turn the dream had kept her going, had kept her making the rounds, waiting on tables, acting in workshops for no pay. She couldn't conceive of life without that goal to work toward. The thought of achieving it thrilled her; that she might lose it frightened her.

The dryer stopped tumbling, and she tried to still her thoughts as she removed her clothes and folded them. There was no use worrying about something that might not even happen—at least not in the near future. If she didn't go to Broadway with the Arc, it might be a long time before she got there on her own steam.

She distracted herself in the afternoon by going to the movies. When she returned, even though she hadn't seen Andy's car on the street, she peeked into the carriage house, but there was no sign of him. Nor was he at the theater when she signed in at half hour. She asked Gretchen about his whereabouts, but she hadn't seen him, either. He didn't show up at intermission, but after the final curtain he surfaced in the dressing room to meet with the anxious cast.

"I'm afraid the news isn't good, people," he began. He recounted the events in Josh Phillips's office. "When I got back I had a long meeting with Gerry. She's grateful to all of you for your work, but feels she can't pass up the opportunity. And I can't see the use in holding her back because the Phillips Organization is short-sighted and motivated by money. I know this is a disappointment to you all. I'm sorry."

No one spoke for a moment, and all Joy could think about was the limousine she'd imagined the night before. Now it was pulling away from the curb, leaving her behind.

"Will the Arc get something out of this, financially I mean?" Harvey asked.

"Yes. According to our contract with the playwright, Phillips will have to pay us a percentage. And we'll get credit in the program as the original producers. But it doesn't make the pill any easier for me to swallow," Andy said bitterly.

"Console yourself by making good use of the money, Andy," Lila suggested.

"Yeah," Sarah put in, "pay us more than scale."

They all laughed weakly and settled glumly in their chairs.

"If everyone's going to look like this," Mark said dryly, "we ought to hold a proper wake. Go over to the parish house, order in some pizzas, drink up the wine that's left from the party. Make ourselves good and miserable."

"I second the motion," Ken said.

The news had grabbed Joy like an icy hand; she had to do something to rid herself of the chilling apprehension that was settling over her. She jumped to her feet. "What are we waiting for?" she cried, and led the gang next door where they proceeded to hold revels that would have put many an Irishman to shame.

9

LUCKILY JOY WAS IN THE OFFICE the morning the Phillips Organization phoned her and was able to field the call herself. If Andy or Gretchen, even Janet, had answered the phone, the news would have been all over the theater. This way she could keep her audition secret. No one need know that on Monday, when there was no performance, she was taking the train into New York to read for the Broadway production of *Sisters and Daughters*. She would just say that she had a few things to take care of in the city.

The Phillips fiasco was a sore point with the company, especially with Andy, and if it was known that she had been approached by Josh Phillips there would be bad feeling all around. When the call had come, Joy had examined her loyalties, but she knew that she couldn't pass up the chance to audition. If they were looking for name players, it was unlikely they would hire her anyway, but she couldn't deny herself the opportunity to read for one of Broadway's most important producing organizations. She hated the thought of skulking around, of not saying anything to Andy, but after their heated discussion a few nights back over why he hadn't accepted Phillips's offer to direct the play, she felt he wouldn't be as charitable toward her desire to advance her career as he had been to Gerry Westover's.

He had been pressing her every day to stay on after the show closed at the end of the coming week, but she still hadn't been able to make a decision. If there had been a part for her in the next production, perhaps her choice would have been easier. As satisfying as she found being involved in the administration of the theater, she was an actress first and foremost. She didn't want to hang around the Arc waiting until there was a part that was right for her. She wanted to be doing something active about finding work for herself. She had tentatively suggested splitting her time between New York and Philadelphia—Tuesday through Thursday in the city, Friday through Monday at the Arc. But Andy wanted all or nothing, or rather he wanted all without accepting that nothing was the alternative.

She found it wrenching in the intervening days not to say anything to Andy about the audition. And there was no one at the theater she could confide in, no "safe" phone from which to make a call to a friend. It was even worse when she returned after a thrilling audition for Josh Phillips himself and Larry Keynes, a director who had more Broadway hits than fingers, plus a few toes. But her distress became nearly unbearable when she learned one day before the show was to close at the Arc that she was to play Barbara on Broadway.

She wanted to shout with joy, wanted to share her excitement with Andy, but kept her secret to herself, like a mother cat hiding her kittens in the closet where they were born to protect them from harm. She had promised to give Andy her answer about staying or going on closing night. As the final performance drew near, the tension between them grew. They were guarded with each other, careful about what they said and did, as if a false word or deed might bring the fissure that was developing underground to the surface.

During the closing night party they both maintained a superficial level of gaiety, but when they returned to the carriage house Joy could no longer delay the difficult task of telling him not only that she was going but why. Without a fire the room was cold and silent. She shivered, but he took no notice. She put a tentative hand on his arm. "I don't know how to say this, Andy. There probably isn't a good way—"

"You're not staying," he said it for her.

"No."

"I knew it," he said quietly. She thought she'd done well at stashing away her secret, but like kittens in a closet its presence had not gone unnoticed. "What happened in New York on Monday?"

She told him about the audition.

"And you got the part," he said tautly. She nodded. "And you're taking it." She nodded again.

He got up and circled the room, warily, angrily, like a newly caged lion. Finally he sat down beside her again and cupped her chin roughly in his hand. "My own little Benedict Arnold," he growled.

Joy pushed his hand away and moved back from him. "I don't deserve that, Andy, and you know it. Why don't you grow up? I hurt you so you have to hurt me back?"

"What do you expect me to do? Ooze and gush and tell you how happy I am for you? I'm damned hurt and damned angry. You betrayed me, Joy."

"Why you narrow-minded . . . Gerry Westover let Phillips option the play from you. I didn't hear you ranting and raving about her being a traitor," she snapped.

"Gerry Westover hasn't shared my bed for the past two months."

"And because I have I can't further my career the same as Gerry. That's one helluva double standard, Andy."

He leaned back against the sofa and ran his hands slowly through his hair, as if his skull were about to crack and he had to push the pieces back together. "I knew something had happened on Monday," he said quietly, "but it never occurred to me that you'd have anything to do with Phillips. I thought I knew you, Joy. I thought—" He closed his eyes briefly and then looked squarely at her. "I thought I loved you."

"If you could change your mind because I did one thing you don't like, then you must have thought wrong." Only at that moment did Joy realize the high stakes for which she had been playing. She had been willing to risk angering him; now she knew she had lost him. A tight knot of sadness and regret began to form between her breasts.

"Why didn't you tell me about the audition?"

"Because I didn't think you'd understand why I had to go. I was right," she added in a choked whisper. The knot inside her was tying itself into ever more intricate patterns. "Would you have felt differently now if I'd told you?"

"At least you wouldn't have been doing something behind my back," he said defensively.

"I know it doesn't make it right, but I hated that part most of all. I felt I couldn't confide in you and do what I had to do for myself." She cocked her head to one side thoughtfully. "That's pretty sad, isn't it, after all we've been to each other these past two months?"

"Are you going to throw all that away?"

"I don't want to, but I know I can't turn down this job, either. I don't know why you don't understand that, Andy. You ought to. All my life I've had this vision of myself working on Broadway. I can't tell you how many rough spots it's gotten me over. It's the same as you and the Arc. You did whatever you had to do to be true to your vision. Why can't you let me do the same?"

"What do you think you're going to get on Broadway that you're not going to get here? It's just a name, Joy."

"Not to me." She was trying to remain calm, to reason this out with him, but her temper was rising again. "It's what I want, and I'm going to go after it. I'd like to see what you would do if someone tried to tell you not to pursue something you want."

He threw up his hands and said hotly, "All right, go back to New York. Get your Broadway credit. And then where will you be? Back on the street with thousands of other poor schnooks who would sell their souls to get their names on a Broadway marquee."

She gave him a steely look and held on to her composure. How dare he insult her that way? "Maybe I won't be back on the street. Maybe I'll go right to another job and then to another and another after that. But even if I don't at least I'll know I've tried. *You* wouldn't dare to take a risk like that. No. You're too comfortable here where you can control everything. You wouldn't even go and find out what it's like. Josh Phillips gave you the chance and you turned it down flat. Stay here then. Hide behind your self-righteous attitudes."

Andy got up abruptly and stalked the room again. He had an overwhelming sense of déjà vu. He'd been speeding down this road before, careening around the same corners. He forced his temper to a screeching halt. *This is Joy,* he told himself. *A week ago you were thinking of sharing your life with her and now you're pushing her away, trying to tell her she doesn't have the right to make her own mistakes.* He approached the couch slowly from behind and laid his hands gently on her shoulders. "The real reason I want you to stay, Joy, is that I want you to marry me."

Joy sat perfectly still for a long moment, letting the words sink in. The deeper they penetrated the hotter she got. She shrugged his hands off her shoulders and turned on him. "Is that what you really think of me, Andy?" she hissed. "That you can offer me my M.R.S. and I'll remain a willing student at your own personal university? I don't want to get married for the sake of getting married. I want to be with someone who understands me, who's not afraid to let me grow, in my own way, at my own speed. Anyway, I thought you said you were mistaken about loving me."

"I was mistaken. Excuse me," he said sarcastically, "I had a moment of weakness." He perched on the corner of the sofa and leaned toward her. He spoke with deadly quiet. "On that first Saturday we spent together I started thinking about what it would be like to have you here with me all the time. Over the weeks I thought more and more about it and I decided to ask you to marry me. I thought you were the one person who could share the life I've built here. My instincts don't fail me often, but this time—" he shook his head unbelievingly "—they've let me down royally."

"Don't worry about it too much. I won't be a total loss," she said cuttingly. "Next time you'll know it's a good idea to let the other person in on your plans before they get too elaborate." She stood up on surprisingly firm legs and turned in the direction of the stairs. "I have a few things upstairs. I'll get them and go."

She collected her robe, a sweat suit, thonged sandals and toiletries from the loft without really looking at it, pushing away the thoughts of the many hours of happiness, of unbridled passion, she had enjoyed there. Head held high, eyes aimed straight ahead, she descended the stairs. Without glancing at him, she plucked her coat from the chair where she had dropped it. "Goodbye, Andy," she said, and walked out of the room.

The outer door closed with a loud click, and Andy said to the empty room, "Goodbye, Joy." *My joy. My sorrow more likely,* he thought as he stretched out on the couch. He propped up his feet on one arm of the sofa and folded his arms behind his neck.

This was it for him. The hell with "settling down." His parents would have to be happy with whatever grandchildren Jim and Danny supplied. Both times he'd put his heart on the line he'd had a big hole shot into it. And the first empty spot was a pin dot compared to this one. No, he'd save his emotions for his work. From here on he'd stick to safe relationships where he wouldn't end up wounded and hurting. He didn't need this kind of pain.

For one last fruitless minute he waited downstairs, listening for the door to open again. But it didn't. He went up to bed, stripped and climbed in between the sheets. A moment later he was up again to open the windows, not only in the loft but downstairs, too. The whole damn place smelled of her. He had to air it out. He dragged a couple of extra blankets out of the storage closet and threw them on the bed. Despite their added warmth he shivered fitfully through the long cold night, missing the heat of her body, her presence, her glow.

He took the pain stoically; it would pass, like a bad reaction to a typhus shot. In a few days he'd be fit again and ready to move on—but he'd never take the chance of coming down with this painful disease. Never again.

JOY DIDN'T PUT HER COAT ON when she got outside, didn't feel the bone-chilling cold as she walked across the yard toward the back door of the parish house. She went up to her room and began packing. As soon as it was light she would call a cab and go to the station. She worked slowly, methodically, and when she had closed her two large suitcases she pulled a chair up to the window and sat watching the bare branches of the trees, reflected in the glow of the streetlight. She felt just as stripped, just as empty, but unlike the tree she had no assurance that spring would come again for her. Just the opposite—it seemed she was embarking on a bitter interminable winter.

But it was my own choice, she reminded herself. *I didn't have to go. I could have stayed on, married him.* He wasn't the only one who'd had secret plans on the subject; she'd indulged in a few fantasies herself. But harmless fantasies were one thing, real expectations quite another. He had expected everything from her— labor, love, loyalty—and unconditionally, too. She had given all of those things freely until she had reached her own limits. Because of those limits she had lost him; but the alternative was losing herself.

She'd been alone before—was it only two months ago? Somehow she would learn to be alone again, but she knew she would never be the same. Like the tree outside, she might grow other leaves in the spring, but her finest foliage was gone forever.

10

THREE DAYS BEFORE *Sisters and Daughters* was scheduled to begin Broadway previews, Joy dragged herself home from rehearsal by sheer strength of character. It was only a four-block walk from the theater to her apartment building, but she'd been sorely tempted to take a taxi. She convinced herself the fresh air would do her good and trudged sluggishly down Forty-fifth Street.

It wasn't the physical effort of the rehearsals that was getting her down; it was the mental effort. Larry Keynes was a brilliant director, and she had learned an enormous amount from working with him, but he was also impatient and exacting. If an actor didn't interpret a direction perfectly the first time, he made a snide remark; on a second unsuccessful try he cut you down a little further; fail a third time and he slashed at you with a saber-sharp tirade. Not that she was the only one to feel his sting; he treated everyone the same way. Her fellow players didn't seem to mind as much as she did. But they were far more experienced than she—their collective list of credits would stretch halfway across the Atlantic. Their skins seemed to be thicker. Perhaps that came with experience.

Charlotte Piersall, who was playing her half sister Madeline, even seemed to enjoy Larry's manner. Joy thought she sometimes deliberately misinterpreted a direction in order to spar with him, and sometimes Larry went along with the game, giving her ambiguous or even contradictory commands. From afar Charlotte had always been one of Joy's idols. She was a formidable actress, but Joy was learning up close that she also had an outspoken personality and a larger-than-life ego. From the first rehearsals she sought to expand Madeline's already substantial part, and the territory into which she had decided to expand was Joy's. She did this so subtly, though, that it had taken Joy, awed and naive as she was, several days to realize what was going on. Once she did, however, she began to stand up firmly and protect her own position. This at least gained Charlotte's respect, but in no way lessened her determination to put herself in the spotlight as often as possible.

The play itself had changed, too. Joy had counted on the familiarity of a play she had already rehearsed and performed to balance the fact that everyone else involved was an old hand. But Gerry Westover, in her first Broadway outing, was anxious to be accommodating to everyone, from Josh Phillips on down, and the play was no longer the comforting beacon Joy had looked forward to.

She reached her corner, and her aching stomach reminded her she'd had little more than half a soggy tuna sandwich and a couple of cups of cold coffee all day. But she was too weary to deal with shopping and preparing a meal, so she continued on another block and went into the café where she'd been working before going off to the Arc. She hadn't been in since returning from Philadelphia; she'd been very few places since coming back. She didn't seem to have the zest for life she'd once had.

She paused for a moment inside the door. The bar was packed and noisy with the late-afternoon crowd, but on the other side of the room most of the tables were free. The pretheater rush wouldn't start for half an hour. She spotted Chris Owens at the back of the restaurant and took a table at her station.

"Joy!" Chris exclaimed, and bounced over to the table. "How are you? We've all been wondering if we'd see you again—now that you're on your way to fame and fortune."

Joy smiled apologetically. "I've been meaning to drop in, but things have been hectic."

"I should have such problems. But as you can see by my mere presence, I don't. So tell me all about it. What's it like working with Larry Keynes?"

"It's like taking a crash course in everything you ever wanted to know about theater. I can't tell you how much I've learned." Joy knew from Chris's wide-eyed look she wouldn't get much sympathy if she unburdened her real feelings.

"And what about Charlotte Piersall?"

"Charlotte is . . ." Joy paused to choose her words. "She's as big in person as she is on the stage."

"Ahhh," Chris sighed, rubbing her hands together, "do I detect a little 'sibling rivalry'? That's what the play's about, isn't it? I remember seeing the reviews when you opened in Philly." Impulsively she touched Joy's hand. "No, don't tell me. I'd rather have my fantasies about being a star. Gee, it's really good to see you. I can't say I'm not green with envy, but I'm so delighted for you, Joy."

"Thanks, Chris," Joy said, realizing how happy and grateful she was not to be waiting tables anymore, not to be scurrying around to auditions or sitting home hoping the phone would ring. She wouldn't trade places with Chris for anything. "I hope you get what you want soon, too."

"Me, too," Chris said with a big sigh. "Can I get you a drink? Are you waiting for someone?"

"A glass of white wine, please. And, no, I was just too tired to cook. You don't have to bring a menu, Chris. I still know it by heart. If only I knew my lines half as well," she added with a rueful laugh. "Previews start in three days. I'm a little nervous."

"I can understand that."

"Say, would you like to come to a preview? I can get you a couple of house seats," she offered.

"That'd be super!"

Joy sipped her wine and ate a decent meal—broiled bluefish, baked potato and salad—her first in days, and felt herself begin to unwind a little. And think. From the first rehearsal she'd been measuring this experience with *Sisters and Daughters* against that in Philadelphia. *It's my way of holding on to the Arc, and to Andy,* she realized with a start. She did genuinely miss the spirit of cooperation that existed there, and she did genuinely regret that Gerry Westover hadn't been firmer about the rewriting she had been requested to do. The play was more slickly theatrical now; the highs and lows were clearly marked and there were more places where the audience might find its breath taken away. But many of the subtleties that made the play so interesting had been erased in the process. Josh Phillips had been clear that he didn't want the people who bought his high-priced tickets to have to work too hard; they came to the theater to relax, not to get a mental workout.

In that respect Andy had been right. Money did matter too much. There were investors to satisfy and too often decisions were made on that basis. But that didn't make everyone involved venal and short-sighted. They were working under a different set of rules and that influenced their behavior. Very few people in this society, in any society, had the luxury of being unconcerned about money. Even Andy worried about the stuff—winning grants, enlarging his subscription base, increasing ticket sales, finding patrons.

Andy. How she had missed him these six weeks. Winter was waning, and the city showed imminent signs of spring, but she hadn't felt any stirrings of life in her heart. She concentrated on her work, saw friends now and then, but otherwise stayed close to home, not even considering the notion of dating again. Who could there be after Andy?

She finished her meal and ordered tea and a piece of carrot cake. *You have to start getting out more,* she told herself firmly. And not only socially. She had a lot to do about creating momentum in her career. She still didn't have a good agent or the connections she needed to move on after the show closed.

The crowd that had gathered in the restaurant began to thin; it was getting close to showtime. She paid her check, left a generous tip for Chris and on a sudden whim decided to go across the street to Theater Row and get a ticket for a play she'd been wanting to see. Once her own show opened she wouldn't have the chance to get to the theater—not for a good long time, she hoped. Besides, she counseled herself, you never knew who you might run into in the lobby.

THANK HEAVEN FOR PREVIEWS, Joy reflected as she sat in her dressing room on opening night. The thought of going out on that stage tonight was terrifying enough.

Without the previous week of trying out the play before the critics reviewed it, she would have been in a catatonic state rather than merely rigid with fear as she was now.

She had been thrilled to have her first private dressing room, but tonight she missed having someone else around to share these final nervous minutes. The mirror in front of her was plastered with telegrams from family and friends, and there were two bouquets—flowers from her parents and a handful of colorful balloons from her nieces. The latter she had tied to the arm of her chair, and they floated gently a couple of feet above her head.

There was a knock at the door, and when she said, "Come in," the assistant stage manager called the official half hour to her. Vainly she had waited to hear from Andy—a card, a telegram, anything. She needed to know that he wished her well tonight. She had hoped he could have found it in his heart to wish her that much. But nothing else would come backstage now.

Her disappointment was worse, knowing that he would be in the audience this evening. He and the Arc were credited with the original production in the program; it would have been very bad form for him not to show up, although he was so stubborn that she could imagine him refusing the invitation. But yesterday Gerry had made sure to mention to her that he would be coming tonight, not only to the performance but to the party afterward. She hoped they could be at least outwardly civil with each other.

Now stop it, she told herself sharply. *This is not the time to brood over Andy Thornhill. You've done enough of that already.* She did a brief relaxation exercise and began the ritual of her preparations.

Her intimacy with the play carried her through the first scene and turned a skittish start into a competent, adequate one. While waiting in the wings between her first appearance and the second, her fear suddenly left her. She was opening on Broadway; she had attained the goal she'd worked for so long. Why shouldn't she enjoy it to the fullest? Like the motor of a carefully tuned racing car, she suddenly revved up and switched into high gear. When she stepped onto the stage again, she was fully charged and running smoothly.

She ran at the same high rate for the rest of the performance, taking even the most dangerous curves in the play without losing speed or racing too fast but aware that she was always just one hairpin away from calamity—a flubbed line, a loss of concentration, a misfired emotion. But she pulled into the final scene as if she'd been driving the course for years, and at the curtain calls she stepped forward to accept her trophy—the enthusiastic applause of the audience.

She didn't run out of gas until she stepped off the stage after the company's final bows. Her gears stopped meshing, and she lurched to a halt in the wings, causing Charlotte, who was right behind her, to crash into her.

"Sorry," Joy mumbled.

Charlotte put a firm hand under her elbow and steered her out of the path of an approaching stagehand. "I was wondering when you were going to crashland," she said expansively.

"So was I," Joy admitted.

"Ease up, Joy, you did very well for a first-nighter."

"Thanks. Thanks very much." From Charlotte Piersall that was high praise. "The show went well, didn't it?" she asked anxiously.

"I give us five or six weeks. I wouldn't wait too long before lining up something else for yourself. I've already started putting out my feelers." She let go of Joy's arm and pushed her way into the circle surrounding Larry Keynes and Josh Phillips.

Joy hugged and kissed her way through the backstage hubbub to her dressing room, basking in the acclaim and attention. By the time she was alone in her room, the thought of seeing Andy no longer agitated her as it had previously. Her affair with him was over; her time at the Arc was over. Her future, at least professionally, seemed to sparkle before her. She felt powerful, capable, ready to tackle anything—or anyone.

She exchanged her stage makeup for a shimmering nighttime face, brushed her hair into a shining wave and changed into her new dress, a white satin sheath, its plunging neckline edged with rows of iridescent seed pearls. She strapped her feet into pale pink sandals and floated happily to Sardi's, where in a private room above the famous restaurant the opening night party was already in progress.

She stepped off the elevator, walked through a set of glass doors and found herself in a crush of people waiting for drinks at the bar. She tried to pass through it, intent on finding her family, but as soon as she was recognized she was pressed from all sides for handshakes and kisses. Photographers aimed cameras at her from all angles. A television reporter thrust a microphone in her face, and she was nearly blinded by the light behind the Minicam recording her reactions. She wanted to whoop with unbridled delight, but managed to remain slightly more composed for the brief interview.

The applause that greeted her when she entered the main part of the room nearly sent her into a swoon. No one had warned her about it; it was totally unexpected. She clasped her hands in front of her mouth in surprise and then did an impromptu turn and curtsy, garnering a laugh and a second burst of clapping.

She scanned the crowded room quickly and spotted her father's beaming smile. She waved to him and began to weave her way among the tables to her family. Her mother gave her a tearful hug; her father a big smooch as he lifted her off her feet and twirled her around, just the way he had when she was a little girl. When he put her down her sister and brother-in-law each grabbed a hand, and the three of them huddled closely. "We're so proud of you," her sister enthused.

The welcome she had enjoyed was repeated for each of the principals as they entered the room. Charlotte made sure she was the last to arrive and gave a grandstand entrance. She behaved like royalty and was received as if she were.

"I know I'm prejudiced," Mrs. Kingsley said to Joy, "but I thought you were every bit as good as she was."

"You're a pal, Mom," Joy said, thrilled to hear genuine approbation in her mother's voice, "but I've got a few things to learn before I get to Charlotte's level." *And not only about acting,* she thought. *I was as gawky as a child at a school prize ceremony when I came in tonight.* So much was opening up for her; it was hard to take it all in.

Her father got a glass of champagne for her, and the family drank a toast to her and to the success of the play. A meal was served, but Joy hardly ate a bite or tasted the few morsels she put in her mouth. Her head was too far into the clouds to pay attention to so merely mortal an occupation as eating.

Her family left directly after the meal, citing the three-hour drive back to Connecticut as the reason for leaving so early, but Joy suspected they wanted to give her the chance to enjoy the rest of the evening with her friends and colleagues, without feeling obligated to entertain them. She walked them to the elevator, kissed them all good-night and wished them a safe drive home. "Thank you all so much for everything," she gushed, feeling suddenly mushy and sentimental, "driving down and the flowers and balloons and for putting up with me and sticking with me. I know I haven't pleased you all the time, but I hope you realize now why I had to do what I did." Her eyelids began to flutter over the small wall of water that threatened to spill over, and between blinks she noticed that even her father's upper lip was quivering a little. She hugged them all again and waved until the elevator door closed and they were gone.

She returned to the party, feeling a little sad that her family could so applaud her success and yet have been less than approving of her struggle to achieve it. But then how could she—or anyone—expect others to have faith in a dream that was so hard to understand and so risky.

"Hello, Joy." The familiar voice plucked her out of her thoughts and set her vibrating like a violin string.

She turned toward the sound and saw him. "Andy," she said quietly. He seemed thinner than when she'd last seen him, and older, though less than three months had passed since then. But he was no less handsome, the blaze in his eyes no less intense. "You're looking well," she said.

"So are you. Fame and fortune agree with you."

There was a cutting edge to his voice, and she looked away. "I'm hardly rich and famous."

"You will be after the reviews tomorrow. You created quite a sensation tonight. Every other conversation I hear is about you. Haven't you noticed?"

"No, I haven't." She kept her voice level, but she wanted to shout at him, *Why can't you simply be civil? Why do you have to try to hurt me? Haven't we hurt each other enough?*

He dropped his eyes for a moment, as if he had read her thoughts. "You deserve it, Joy. You were very good tonight. Congratulations."

"Thank you." She knew the compliment wasn't an empty one. If he hadn't admired her performance, he wouldn't have said anything.

"The play isn't what it was, is it?"

"No, it isn't," she snapped, "and no thanks to you." He had no right to criticize what had happened to the play. He'd walked away from the chance to be involved.

"Me? What do I have to do with it?"

"Nothing. That's just the point. If you'd taken up Josh Phillips's offer to direct, this wouldn't have happened. You wouldn't have let it. But, no, you couldn't risk getting your hands dirty in the real world." As soon as the words were out of her mouth, she regretted them. She looked at him aghast and watched his face harden.

"I hope you get what you want from life, Joy," he said in a rough voice. He made a quick pivot and started away from her.

"Andy!" She took a step after him and put a hand on his arm. He looked down coldly at it, but she wasn't deterred. "Wait," she said softly. "This isn't right. We can't treat each other this way."

"Can't we?" he said gruffly before his face crumbled. "I'm sorry. I guess there're still a lot of feelings left—for both of us."

"Yes," she agreed. "I miss you," she went on bravely. "I think about you a lot."

"Do you?" he asked, surprised and pleased.

"Of course. Just because we parted ways doesn't mean I've forgotten you."

"I've tried to forget you." He smiled sheepishly. "I haven't done very well."

"No?" Her heart began to make spectacular jumps and leaps like a Russian folk dancer.

"No."

They looked at each other for a long moment, possibilities buzzing busily around their heads like a swarm of bees, both wanting the honey, both afraid to be stung.

"Are you going to be in town long?" she asked. Maybe if they could have lunch tomorrow, see each other in a neutral setting . . .

"I was planning to start back soon, but . . ." For a selfish reason—not wanting to come alone—he'd brought Gretchen with him, even knowing she might read more than he wanted her to into the gesture. Asking her to drive back to Philadelphia alone would be thoughtless. "Maybe we could slip out for a few minutes now."

As much as she wanted to see him she didn't want to leave her first ever Broadway opening night party. "Maybe later," she suggested.

They looked at each other hesitantly, still weighing the honey against the stings, unable to make the first foray into the fray. While they were equivocating someone else stepped in.

"There you are, Joy. I've been looking all over for you."

Joy looked uncertainly at the speaker, wondering who was speaking so intimately to her, racking her brain to remember if she'd met the woman somewhere before.

"I'm Sondra Carroll. You and I need to talk."

Joy hoped her amazement didn't show. She'd imagined such a powerful agent to have stature at least equal to her reputation, but Sondra Carroll was barely five feet tall, plumpish and dowdy, with thinning mouse-brown hair and an obvious overbite.

"I'll talk to you another time, Joy," Andy said politely. "Drop in if you're ever in Philadelphia." He drifted away before she could say anything else.

"Who was that?" Sondra Carroll asked bluntly. "Oh, yes," she said dismissively when Joy told her. "I want you to come and see me in my office tomorrow. Say about four?" She eyed Joy's champagne glass. "You probably won't be good for much before then." Before Joy could say anything—yes, no, whatever—Sondra Carroll said, "Don't be late," and disappeared into the crowd.

Quickly Joy drained the final two gulps of champagne from the glass she had been clutching. Heavens, she thought, what else could happen tonight—the opening, her family, Andy, now Sondra Carroll. Her high heels already felt like stilts; one more unexpected encounter and she could easily lose her balance.

"We can't have you with an empty glass, Joy." Josh Phillips pulled her arm through his and began to steer her toward the bar. "Enjoying yourself? You ought to be."

"I certainly am," she said. "It's been one of the most eventful nights of my life."

At the bar Mr. Phillips got her a fresh glass of champagne and introduced her to one of the show's backers, a smooth-talking businessman who spirited Joy away to meet one of his associates. The associate wanted to introduce her to someone else, and she was handed around to several groups who seemed anxious not only to meet her but to keep her glass filled. She couldn't decide what threatened the size of her head more—the endless supply of champagne or the compliments. There was little she could do about the compliments except to accept them graciously, but after the first couple of refills she used her glass more as a prop than a drinking vessel and took only small judicious sips now and again.

But she had a strong impulse to drain the glass when she happened to glance at the door and saw Andy walking through it with his arm around Gretchen Weiler's waist. *Oh, stop it,* she told herself firmly. *Just because you've been carrying the torch for him doesn't mean he has to carry it for you.* Still, it hurt to see him touching someone else, especially after the way they had looked at each other earlier. *You could have stayed with him,* she reminded herself. *And miss this?* She looked around the room at all the well-known people, listened to the animated chatter, the clink of glasses. *Not on your life, Andy Thornhill,* she vowed, and downed a great gulp of bubbly wine. And then another and another until her glass was empty.

Someone soon put a full glass in her hand, and she drank it quickly. The wine loosened her tongue and her inhibitions. She made several jokes and reveled in the merry laughter they produced. Her senses seemed to grow sharper and clearer—forms were distinct even in the dim light; she could pick up snatches of conversations from all directions; the mixture of smoke and warm perfume pricked her nostrils; her tongue tingled with each taste of champagne. Then suddenly the room and everyone in it began to come apart. It was like looking at a painting melt; all the colors ran together into an indistinct blob. She teetered uncertainly and blinked rapidly, trying to reverse the flow. Finally the sensible part of her took charge, and she excused herself and dashed to the lounge.

The trouble with drowning your sorrows, she thought when she had calmed down, *is that you drown yourself along with them.* And though she didn't want to feel the pain caused by seeing Andy again, she had no desire to go down the drain with it. Gradually, her panic passed, and she repaired her hair and makeup, preparing to return to the party. She couldn't go home until the reviews were in and that wouldn't be for hours. Until then she vowed to drink only club soda and to stop playing for laughs.

The party broke up at dawn and Joy, feeling more than a bit like Cinderella after the ball, was taken home in a chauffeured limousine. Although her personal notices were glowing, the mixed reviews for the play had dampened everyone's spirits, including her own. With luck the play might run a couple of months, but she'd be out of work soon enough. Maybe not for long, she told herself brightly, if things went well with Sondra Carroll.

But it would be a long time before she fell in love again. She knew that with more certainty than she'd

known anything. Her feelings for Andy ran deep, like
a silent underground stream that flowed back upon itself because it had no outlet. She'd grown used to that
dammed-up feeling over the weeks, but now the stream
was freshly fed and rushing hard at the barriers that restrained it.

Mercifully the limo stopped in front of her building.
She stumbled up to her apartment and fell into bed, exhausted, too tired to do anything but fall into a deep
dreamless sleep.

ANDY SAT UP ALL NIGHT thinking about her, thinking
how beautiful she had looked, thinking how much he
had wanted her. He regretted his stinging words, regretted his anger. But it was there, standing beside his
love for her, a matched set; he couldn't separate them.

How empty it was here without her, and not only in
his bed. He missed finding her at his desk in the office,
missed her at the theater. So many of the simple plea-
sures he'd taken for granted were ruined by memories
of her. He couldn't look at an Eakins painting, shop at
the Reading Terminal Market or eat a cheese steak
without thinking of her. But the worst thing was the
gnawing hunger deep inside him, a hunger that nothing could satisfy.

There seemed to be no solution to the problem. She
was taking New York by storm; he was taking care of
the Arc. She'd never be happy here; he'd never been
happy there. Somehow he had to find a way to get her
out of his system; he couldn't go on like this.

11

PROMPTLY AT FOUR THE NEXT DAY Joy rang the buzzer outside Sondra Carroll's locked office and identified herself to the voice that came over the small intercom. She couldn't count the times she'd stood in front of similar intercoms in similar hallways, trying to get in to see an agent. Very few actors succeeded in getting past the security systems that were installed principally to keep them out. How odd that would seem to most businesses—locking the door to keep out potential clients. But today she had been summoned. This door would open.

"If you want to leave a picture and résumé, slip it under the door."

"I have an appointment," she informed the bored voice. She wondered how many times a day the same message was broadcast into this hallway.

"You do? Just a minute," the annoyed reply came back.

A full minute later the buzzer sounded releasing the lock, and Joy opened the door.

"Sorry. Sondra forgot to tell me about you." The voice belonged to a young man wearing black pleated trousers, white shirt, thin black tie and bright aqua shoes. A tiny gold earring glittered in his right earlobe. "I'm Duncan, Sondra's assistant. She'll be with you sometime. Have a seat." He waved a hand toward a shabby brown armchair. "I know the place is a dump, but Sondra—" he lowered his voice "—has no eye for decor—interior or personal. But, thank the goddess, that's not what she's paid for. Can I get you some coffee? I promise you it's not as old as the chair."

"No, thanks," Joy said with a smile. The office was indeed as unprepossessing as Sondra Carroll herself. The dapper Duncan looked out of place among the crumbling mountains of pictures and résumés, the dusty back issues of the *Player's Guide*, the ancient mud-green filing cabinets.

"When I first took the job I tried to spruce it up a bit, but I got to feel like the little Dutch boy. You can only hold your finger in the dike for so long."

The door to Sondra Carroll's office was closed, and she could hear muffled words. Five minutes passed, then ten; after fifteen minutes Joy began to get impatient. She was about to say something to Duncan when the door flew open.

"Come in," Sondra Carroll commanded Joy. "Hold the phones, Duncan, until I'm finished."

Opposite Sondra's cluttered desk was a chair identical to the one in the outer office. Joy took it, and Sondra started the interview while digging through the top drawer of a filing cabinet behind her desk. On tiptoes she could just about see into the top of it. "Why haven't I seen you before?" she demanded.

"I've tried to see you," Joy said. "I could never get in the front door, or past the receptionist on the phone."

Sondra pulled out a file folder and slapped it on top of an already teetering pile on the desk. She laughed gruffly and sat in her chair. "I didn't necessarily mean in the office. I meant onstage."

"Because I haven't done very much—at least here in town." Joy found Sondra's brusque manner unbalancing, a bit bewildering. She had never met anyone with less personal charm; nevertheless, Sondra had made her way to the top of a business that relied heavily on personality.

"And because you don't have an agent."

"I'm not signed with anyone. I have informal relationships with a couple of people." She named the agents she had worked with in the past.

Sondra shook her head disparagingly. "No wonder," she muttered darkly. She rummaged in her desk, pushing aside papers, unmindful of the ones that fell on the floor, and pulled out a crumpled sheet. She shoved it across the desk at Joy. "These are the people I'd like you to see. And to see the show."

Joy read quickly down the list of producers and directors. She'd give her eye teeth to meet any one of them, much less all of them. Sondra Carroll might not have charm, but she obviously worked hard and knew what she was doing.

"We'll start with theater first, then move into film and television. I had Josh's office send over your pictures from their files. They're not bad, but I like to start fresh with new clients. They're too girl-next-door. We'll get you something more sophisticated, sassier." She named a photographer she frequently used and told Joy to set up an appointment with him. "Duncan has the number. What about singing and dancing?"

"I'm no Shirley MacLaine," Joy said honestly, "but I can put over a song and learn a routine."

"That's good enough. I'll put some musical people on that list. If I didn't think you were star material, Joy, you wouldn't be sitting here. I only work with stars. I don't have any time for temperamental 'artistes.' This is a business. If you don't want to earn money acting, you can leave now."

"I don't mind paying the rent," Joy answered.

"Good. I don't mind paying mine, either. But just remember if you don't pay your rent, I don't pay mine. Understood?"

Joy nodded and said yes.

Sondra opened and closed a couple of desk drawers before taking out a legal-sized piece of paper. "This is my standard client agreement. I start with a six-month term, renewable if both of us agree. Read this over and I'll have Duncan type one up for you."

As she read the agreement it occurred to Joy that, as she was in a position to shop around for an agent, she ought to do so. But Sondra Carroll had come to her. There had to have been other agents in the audience opening night; others must have read the reviews. But only Sondra Carroll had approached her. Besides, it was only for six months, why shouldn't she sign with one of the best agents in the business?

FOR THE NEXT THREE WEEKS no day passed for Joy without an appointment set up by Sondra to see a producer, director or casting agent. She met people in their offices, a few invited her to lunch, and she did several readings. Then the closing notice went up for *Sisters and Daughters*, and Sondra really got down to business. Joy's schedule was even more hectic, but when the show closed a week later, though she had several irons in the fire, none of them was hot enough to make a brand.

This time, however, Joy joined the ranks of the unemployed almost gleefully. She had an agent that was working hard for her, money in the bank and enough weeks of work to draw a small unemployment check. After the whirlwind winter and spring, she was looking forward to a short breather.

The first four days after closing were spent in Connecticut, lolling in the sun and drinking in the fresh mid-May air and the scent of late-blooming lilacs. She returned to the city refreshed and energized. And a good thing she was, for Sondra had been busier than ever.

"Have I got just the thing for you," she said when Joy checked in with her on her return. "A new musical called *Three-Ring Circus*. The featured role is a guaranteed Tony nomination."

"A musical?"

"You sing for them on Friday. I'm putting you on to Duncan. He'll give you all the details."

Joy was about to protest that she couldn't be prepared in two days—it was already Wednesday morning—but the hold button clicked and Sondra was gone. Seconds later Duncan came on the line. She jotted down the time and place of the audition and what she had been asked to prepare, frowning deeply as she wrote. She hadn't sung since *Pie in the Sky* had closed over a year ago.

She flipped through her address book and immediately put in a call to a vocal coach she had worked with and made appointments for a practice session that afternoon, one on Thursday and another just before the audition on Friday. Then she went to the bottom shelf of her bookcase and sorted through her sheet music. None of the songs she knew seemed suitable, so she picked up her purse and spent the rest of the morning browsing in the music shops on Broadway.

On Friday afternoon she arrived at the theater knowing she had done as much as she could to prepare. With her coach's help, she had picked two songs that were fun to sing, and not too difficult musically, and she went into the audition with the attitude that she'd have as good a time as she could and then go off to the Berkshires for the weekend with an old friend from college. She didn't think she sang particularly well, but all in all she felt she hadn't done badly, considering it was her first musical audition in a long while.

Maybe it was her throwaway attitude, but when she returned on Monday morning there was a message that she had a callback for *Three-Ring Circus* the next day. Besides singing her two songs again, she read from the script and learned one of the numbers from the show. She wasn't overly impressed by either the story line or the music. The script read like a warmed-over situation comedy that hadn't been awfully funny the first time around, and the music sounded like a pastiche of songs from every musical she'd ever heard, everything from *My Fair Lady* to *Cats*. Nor did she think much of the body-jolting, muscle-kinking dance routine the choreographer led her through. She couldn't see why Sondra was so high on this project, but then Sondra had been in the business long enough to know a good script when she saw one. Maybe it would come alive in performance. Some shows were like that—nothing on paper but terrific onstage.

She left the theater thinking she would be happy to see *Three-Ring Circus* pitch its tent without her, but to her great surprise Sondra phoned two days later and said she'd been offered the part.

"I'm not sure I want it," Joy said.

"What do you mean you don't want it? It's a nifty little show. I meant what I said about the Tony nomination."

Sondra sounded ominous, and Joy asked with trepidation, "Are you sure they want me? I didn't think the auditions went all that well."

"They want you," she said emphatically. "I made sure of that."

Joy paused for a moment. "Did you twist someone's arm about this, Sondra? I appreciate all you're doing, but—"

"So the producer owed me a favor. So what? If they didn't really want you, it wouldn't have mattered. Look, Joy, do you want to work or not?"

"Of course I do. Can I think this over?"

"What's to think over? Do you want it or not?"

"Okay," Joy acquiesced, though she was not at all comfortable with Sondra's bullying. But she didn't want to antagonize the only agent in New York who had shown faith in her talent. And Sondra had been knocking herself out for a month.

"Rehearsals begin at the end of June. Out-of-town tryouts start the end of July in Washington, then Baltimore and Philadelphia. You open here the first week of September. Tomorrow you go into training—singing lessons, vocal coaching, dance classes, the works. I'll pay for everything now and deduct it from your salary when you have one. Duncan will fill you in."

So much for the unemployment line, Joy thought uneasily as she waited for Duncan to pick up. "Join the circus and see the world," she muttered to herself. Except that this world included Philadelphia, a place that had been gouged out of her personal globe. Well, he had told her to drop in if she was ever in town. Maybe she'd take him up on his offer. *Oh, Andy,* she thought, *why aren't you here now? I need somebody to talk to about this. I don't know if I'm doing the right thing, but I don't know what else to do.*

"I just heard the joyful noise, love. Congratulations. I adore it when someone gets a job. Sondra's actually in a good mood for half an hour."

"Thanks, Duncan," she replied with a laugh. After Sondra's abruptness, Duncan's acerbic humor was more than welcome.

"Here's the schedule for Camp Carroll. That's camp as in boot, love. This routine would run a marine ragged. I wouldn't want to be in your ballet slippers for the next five weeks." He started to read rapidly down a list of dates and times, names and numbers.

"Slow down, Duncan. I can't write that fast," she begged.

He started again from the top, slowly this time.

12

JOY HAD ALWAYS ABSORBED knowledge the way a sponge sucks up water, and she began her training sessions with a burst of energy and enthusiasm. Still, for the first time since a compulsory biology lab course in college, she was not learning because of a natural desire to grow, but in order to fit herself into a role. It was like changing her body to suit a dress instead of altering the dress.

Her teachers were all excellent, but they had been told by Sondra—who was paying them and from whom they wanted other referrals—to turn Joy into a musical comedy performer. And that went against the grain. She had worked hard to cultivate a realistic, understated style of performing, and these teachers were asking her to do exactly the opposite. The more she studied, the greater the conflict between her instincts and the new technique became. She made strides—her voice became stronger and fuller, her body well-toned and responsive—but she often felt as if someone had grafted an extra arm onto her, one that was awkward and a hindrance to her normal movements.

Four weeks of nearly nonstop dance classes, singing lessons and vocal coaching left her more than ready to start rehearsals. She felt confident she could handle almost any demand that might be made on her, and she was looking forward to a change of pace.

The pace did change—it went from hectic to frenetic. There was no easing into the rehearsals as there had been with *Sisters and Daughters*, no days spent sitting in chairs reading and discussing the script. The cast jumped right into *Three-Ring Circus*, learning music and dance routines, blocking scenes with scripts in hand. The blocking—movements on the stage by the characters—was complicated by the elaborate set design.

The show was about a group of eccentric circus performers whose small traveling tent show has just gone out of business, and there were to be trapezes, trampolines, poles, ladders and chutes. But none of that would be available until the final weeks of rehearsal, so the performers had to mime the moves. Joy spent a lot of mental effort trying to remember whether she was climbing on this line, bouncing on that or swinging on another, especially since so many of the moves assigned by the director seemed arbitrary to her.

She thought it would be easier once she knew the lines, but as soon as she learned them the author was called in for rewrites. She thought it would get better once the set was installed, but it threw off all the timing and the actors spent days scrambling around the stage like a bunch of kids on a new jungle gym.

She felt less than ready to face an audience when the sets, costumes, lights and performers were packed into buses and trucks for the first leg of their out-of-town tryouts. The show hit Washington in the midst of a steamy heat wave, and the audience response was as sluggish as the air outside the theater. So there were more rewrites, and songs were taken out, then put back in. And a new choreographer was brought in, which meant the dance numbers were either cut or reworked.

The troupe trudged on to Baltimore, the heat wave following them. The city and the theater were different, but they seemed to have attracted the same yawning audiences. The cut and paste work continued apace. Everyone, including Joy, was cranky, discouraged and just plain pooped. She began to wish secretly that the show would close out of town, that they would never make it to New York. The show had taken so much out of her and had given so little back. The feeling grew stronger when they arrived in Philadelphia, where she had once had so much.

Her thoughts turned to Andy from the moment the company bus pulled into town. Knowing that he was only a few minutes' drive from her Center City hotel made her think of him even more than she usually did. She began to hope he would show up at the theater one night during their week's run. Her name was in the advertisements that were running in the Philadelphia papers. He might notice it and come to see her. One night after the show, when the stage manager said there was someone asking for her, she thought he had. But she was disappointed to find Mark Curran at the stage door. She was glad to see his familiar face, but it wasn't the one she ached to see.

Each day she toyed with dropping in at the Arc to see him; each night she waited in vain for him to appear at the theater. But the last tryout performance ended, and there was no Andy. There was also no closing notice, and it looked as if the producers were going to open the show in New York. She went to bed frazzled, dejected and unsure how much more she could take. The next day, sitting on the company bus waiting for it to leave for New York, she could take no more. She couldn't go back home feeling this way. She had to see Andy, had to talk to him. She asked one of the actors who lived in her building to take care of her luggage and hopped off the bus. A minute later she was in a taxi heading for the Arc.

She hesitated as she got out of the cab, almost asked the driver to wait, but brushed her fears aside and shut the door with a decisive bang. The worst he could do was tell her to go away. At least she would have tried. And he had told her to drop in if she was in town. She went through the alley between the parish house and the theater and slowly approached the carriage house. As she walked down the narrow passageway, she thought she had some inkling of how a returning soldier felt after war. Though she had spent only two months in this place, the ground was familiar, solid under her feet. With each step the battles of the past months began to fade.

The door to the office was open, and she was about to walk right in, when she remembered she didn't really belong there. She might not be a welcome visitor. She stopped in front of the door and knocked. "Come on in," she heard Andy call. Her heart tripped over the sound of his voice, but she was propelled toward him. She stepped into the office and up to the door of his living quarters. Andy was sitting on the couch reading the Sunday paper. The remains of breakfast were scattered on the coffee table.

"I was in town so I thought I'd take you up on your offer." He looked up and stared at her in momentary surprise and confusion, then his face went blank. "To drop in," she added nervously. Her discomfort increased when Gretchen came into her line of vision carrying a steaming pot of coffee. She looked at the coffee table again and noticed now that there were far too many dishes for one person. "I'm sorry," she stammered. "I didn't—"

"You never do, Joy," Gretchen said acidly. Andy looked at her sharply, and she put the pot down on the table. "I've got some things to do at the theater." She gave Andy a glare and hurried past Joy. The screen door closed with a bang.

"I should have called first," Joy said miserably. She had made a terrible mistake coming here. She had assumed that Andy would be sitting here waiting for her—alone. But he was neither waiting nor alone. The humid air hung on her like a sodden blanket; beads of perspiration broke out on her brow and forehead. "I'll go," she mumbled, and made a quick pivot.

"Don't," he blurted, and sprang up from the couch. She stopped in midstep. "At least stay for a cup of coffee," he finished lamely. Since the day she'd left him he'd been trying to forget her, first with casual dates, then by spending more and more time with Gretchen, even though he knew deep down that she wanted more from him than he'd ever be able to give her. The mere sight of Joy made him see how shabby and ineffective his efforts had been.

Joy turned to him slowly. "I won't stay long. I know you have other things to do." It was the closest she could come to saying she knew there was no place for her here anymore.

"Sit down. I'll get you a mug."

He returned with the one that had been her favorite. At first her heart leaped with delight, the way a lost traveler's would at the sight of a road sign. But then she thought it was probably the first one that had come to hand. She sat down stiffly and took the coffee from him, careful not to touch him as the mug changed hands.

"So, how's it going?" he asked.

"Okay," she replied. "How's everything here?"

"Fine. Getting ready for the fall season. The theater's dark until the middle of September, but there's still a lot to do."

"There always is." Behind their stilted words she could feel crosscurrents as strong as the winds that gathered between skyscrapers and threatened to knock pedestrians off their feet. His next words hit her with a heady gust.

"I knew you were in town, Joy." He couldn't stand this pussyfooting around any longer. "I saw it in the papers, and Mark told me he'd seen the show."

"Then you must know the real reason I'm here." The force between them propelled her to honesty. "Everything's not okay. Everything's lousy."

"I'm sorry," he said. "I mean that."

"I know you don't say things you don't mean." She looked down into her lap. The hurts and disillusionments of the past months were shaking inside her, rumbling like the first warning of an avalanche. She fought hard to hold it back, but time and gravity were against her. The feelings had been building for too long; they had to spill over. "Oh, hell," she swore. "It isn't at all the way I thought it would be."

"Tell me about it," he said gently.

She told him everything—about Sondra nudging her into the contract for *Three-Ring Circus*, about the weeks that had seemed like boot camp, about the confounding changes in the show, the lackluster tryout tour. "The show has no internal integrity, Andy. Whatever honest impulses there were in the beginning are gone. The collaborators are so worried about what 'works' they've forgotten what they want to say or why they want to say it. It's like a body without bones. And I'm the limp middle toe." She gave a rueful laugh.

"You've got a backbone, even if the show doesn't. Why don't you quit?"

"I signed a contract. I'll finish what I started," she said glumly.

"And then go back for more. You're a glutton for punishment, Joy. And not just your own."

"What are you getting at?" she asked warily.

"Five months ago you left me and the Arc and here you are back again. What do you really want, Joy? What are you doing here?"

"You know how it is when you're out on tour," she said defiantly. "I was lonely. I wanted someone to talk to, someone who knew me. I thought maybe enough time had passed for us to be friends. Enough time will never pass, Andy. I know that now." She stood and backed away from the couch.

She got as far as the door to the office when she felt his arms surround her. He turned her toward him, and his mouth pressed against hers in a searing kiss. He held her tighter and tighter, crushing her to him, his mouth burning hers. She resisted him, but her lips were like dry kindling, and she soon caught his fire. There was passion and longing in the kiss, anger and release, but not a touch of tenderness. She did not want him this way; she went limp.

He pushed her away. "Isn't that what you wanted? Isn't it why you came here?"

"No, it isn't."

"Then why? You have friends, family you can talk to. You don't need me. What do you want?" he goaded.

"Nothing very much. Just this." She put her arms around him and leaned her head lightly on his chest, not demanding anything as he had of her. She held him and stroked his back. Every muscle in it was rigid, contracted; his arms were stiff at his sides. "I miss you," she said in a small voice. Warm tears trickled down her cheeks. She held on to him gently, only seeking and giving comfort. Gradually his muscles began to relax, the tempo of his breathing increasing as his heartbeat accelerated.

He rested his cheek on the top of her head. Her hair was warm and silky, fragrant, fresh. They didn't have to hurt each other anymore; they could start again and stay together this time. "My Joy," he whispered, and wrapped his arms around her. "How I've missed you. How I've longed for you to come to me."

"I'm here, Andy. Right here."

He put a gentle hand beneath her chin and raised her face to his. "Where you belong." He smiled and brushed aside her tears, then scooped her up in his arms and carried her up the stairs to the loft. He put her on the bed and knelt beside her. His hand went to the top button on her blouse.

She stayed his hand. "Do you really want *me*, Andy—not some idea of me, not to get back at me, just *me*, with all my faults and quirks?"

"I want what's in here—" he touched her forehead "—and here—" he put his hand over her left breast "—and here." He pressed his palm against her solar plexus, where the soul is said to reside. "I want this," he continued, tousling her hair. "And these." He wiggled the toes sticking out of her open sandals. "And everything in between."

She laughed giddily as he removed her sandals and ran his fingers up and down the soles of her feet. He kissed each toe and nibbled his way up the inside of her legs, reaching up to unfasten the belt and buttons of her skirt and blouse. For months there had been a dull ache deep inside her, and as he undressed her she realized it was wanting him that had nagged at her so.

He undressed quickly and slid into bed next to her. She let out a heavy sigh as he took her into his arms. "What is it, love?"

"I've felt so empty without you," she whispered.

They hugged each other tight, Andy luxuriating in the warmth and softness of her curves, Joy in the strength and heat of his body. Their first caresses were tentative. They needed to get used to each other before giving in to the vivid swirl of emotions their reunion had caused.

But it was not long before their touches took on a demanding urgency. He bent his head to her breast and took the nipple in his mouth. He suckled at it, flicked it with his tongue, felt it engorge, felt a surge in himself he could barely control. At her urging he guided himself into her. She was warm and soft as a tropical sea, and he floated easily on top of her, happy to let her gentle waves take him where they would.

With physical union their reunion was now complete for Joy. She had thought she remembered everything about their lovemaking, but the feel of him was more exquisite than anything she recalled feeling before. He seemed to be sinking into her, reaching an uncharted cove, a private place that existed only for them.

Playfully they explored the place together, rocking back and forth, splashing in and out of the warm, sun-dappled sea that surrounded them, that was them, laughing, exchanging caresses and kisses. A gentle tide buoyed them, and they moved together in a soothing, rocking rhythm. Joy drifted along lazily on the rolling waves of pleasure. With each ebb and flow of sensation, she felt herself grow more open and relaxed, more receptive, more in need of him.

Andy shifted and settled more deeply inside her. Suddenly the tide grew stronger, more forceful. Great crests of feeling swelled and subsided within her, each peaking higher and higher. Each wave of ecstasy threatened to send her tumbling over the edge, but she held back and stopped short of the top each time. She wanted to stretch out this exquisite agony forever. But Andy would have his way. "Come with me, love," he urged, and pressed her to him.

He looked into her eyes, and she could resist him no more. She took a breath and arched to meet the stroke that sent them tumbling into a wild thrashing surf. The waves subsided slowly, and they lay quietly in each other's arms, sated, enjoying the sun-drenched shore they had reached together.

"If I hadn't missed you so," he said after a while, "I'd say that was almost worth the wait."

She put a finger to his lips. "Nothing is worth being apart like we were."

"I said almost." He kissed each finger of the hand she had brought to his face; even the smallest part of her was precious.

"I can't imagine how we managed to stay apart for so long." She ran her hand across his chest, needing to touch him to make sure she wasn't dreaming this moment.

"We're both pretty stubborn."

"I guess so."

He dropped a kiss on her cheek. "It doesn't matter now. We're both here. Together. Thank you for coming, Joy. It took guts."

"No, it took guts to let me stay, especially since—" She was about to mention Gretchen but thought better of it. Things were sticky enough without bringing up anything that might have happened since she'd gone. That was his business. But Andy had realized what she'd been about to say.

"I've been spending some time with Gretchen, Joy, but it's been day time, or evening time, never night time."

She closed her eyes briefly. "You didn't have to tell me that, but I appreciate it. With everything else I wouldn't want—"

He silenced her with a kiss. "Hush now," he said softly. He snuggled close to her, and they dozed off in the midday heat.

ANDY WOKE feeling hot and sticky. Joy was breathing evenly, but her face was covered with a light film of perspiration. The carriage house was cozy most of the year, but during a heat wave it could get close. He ran a hand down her body, and she stirred and opened her eyes slowly. "Want to go swimming?"

She pushed her hair back from her forehead. "Sounds heavenly, but unless you have the bathtub in mind maybe we shouldn't. I don't have a suit with me."

"There must be something you can wear in the costume shop."

They washed and dressed quickly and crossed the yard to the theater. Andy tried the door and found it locked. *Good,* he thought, *Gretchen must have gone off somewhere.* He had long sensed that her feelings for him could be easily encouraged, and it had been weak of him to give her even the little encouragement that he had. But he was glad not to have to deal with it right at this moment. He unlocked the door and groped for the light switch.

Joy followed him in. "It's strange to see the theater empty."

"It doesn't pay to stay open in August, and it gives me a chance to spruce up and catch up."

"And take a vacation once every ten years or so?" she suggested wryly as they went down to the costume shop.

"I'll have you know I'm off to New Hampshire next week. A friend from Yale runs a summer theater up there."

"Talk about a busman's holiday!"

"I'm not going to do anything," he protested.

"Except maybe sit in on a few rehearsals, go to see a couple of shows, read a few scripts this friend just happens to have lying around," she said with a laugh.

He caught her in a close embrace. "Will it help if I promise to go out and sit under a tree every day and do nothing but think of you?"

"It might help you," she said emphatically. "And I don't think I'd mind too much," she added softly.

He let go of her and went to one of the metal cupboards against the far wall. "To be honest, it won't be much different from what I do every day. I think of you a lot, Joy," he said as he rummaged through the shelves.

"I think about you too, Andy." She went up behind him and put her arms around his waist. "Sometimes I talk to you, too."

He turned to her and draped his arms over her shoulders. "You can talk to me in person now." He kissed her lightly and turned back to his task. "This should do," he said, producing a black tank-style leotard.

They collected towels and Andy's swimming trunks and walked the few blocks to the university gym. As an alumnus Andy was entitled to purchase a pass to use the sports facilities. At the entrance he showed his membership card and paid a small guest fee for Joy.

"Last one in is a rotten egg," he said as they went off to their separate locker rooms.

Joy looked for Andy when she emerged from the changing room but didn't see him. She sat down on the edge of the pool to wait, but the water looked too inviting. Half the Olympic-size pool was divided into lanes for serious lap swimmers, the other half left free for recreational swimmers. She picked an empty lane, donned the swimming cap she had borrowed from the locker-room attendant and plunged into the pool. It was shockingly cool, and she felt her body temperature decrease a degree or two almost immediately. She settled into a smooth crawl and swam leisurely to the other end. As she touched the edge before starting back, she noticed Andy coming toward her in the next lane. She held on to the side and waited for him.

"Hi there, rotten egg," she teased as he bobbed up out of the water.

"Race you to the other end," he challenged.

"What's the winner get?"

He thought for a moment. "Loser buys dinner."

"You're on."

"Want a head start?"

"Heck, no." She was a strong swimmer. If she poured it on, maybe she could beat him.

"Okay," he said with a shrug. "On the count of three?" She nodded. "Ready?" She nodded again, and he counted off.

Joy pushed off hard from the side of the pool and set her arms paddling in her fastest, steadiest rhythm. She kicked hard with her legs and feet and took breaths on opposite sides every third stroke. For the first quarter of the pool's length she stayed a nose ahead of him. She increased her stroke for the second quarter and managed to keep him from overtaking her. But his arms were too powerful, and at the halfway mark he surged ahead. Despite her best efforts she finished a body length behind him. She surfaced panting and hoisted herself up, hooking her elbows over the edge of the pool. "Looks like you won yourself dinner, buddy."

"It looks that way," he said with satisfaction. "I didn't think I was going to have to work that hard, though," he admitted.

"I just wanted you to work up an appetite."

"Ha!" he scoffed.

They each swam a few more leisurely laps and then played together in the shallow end of the recreational area. Andy did handstands, and Joy tried to teach him some of the water ballet moves she had learned back in high school, like the dolphin and the shark. They got silly, inventing moves and giving them names like clam and oyster and squid. Late in the afternoon, when they finally left the pool, their fingers were wrinkled from staying in the water so long. But they didn't mind because they were cool and utterly relaxed.

Joy showered and dressed and toweled her hair, but didn't dry it; she would let the sun do that outside. They walked back to the Arc and hung up their things in the bathroom.

"I'm starving," she announced. "What do you want to eat? Winner's choice."

"Seafood, of course. What else can you have when you're eating with a mermaid?" He stroked her damp hair; the sun and air had arranged it in gorgeous waves. "You look so beautiful," he whispered. He cupped her face and kissed her softly, then wrapped his arms around her and held her close, very, very close. He kissed her again, saying with his lips everything that words could express only clumsily.

She held on to him, fearing her legs would become as unable to support her as a mermaid's fin. Each time he kissed her, touched her, looked at her, she knew him better, more deeply, more intimately. And yet she knew today was only a sneak preview of what she could know about him.

They went out to the car and drove down to the waterfront where Andy knew of a simple seafood restaurant. They shared a bucket of steamers and filled themselves almost to bursting with broiled flounder, scallops and shrimp, thick french fries and mounds of vinegary coleslaw, all washed down with frosty mugs of beer. After dinner they strolled along the waterfront until the bright summer light began to fade. On the ride back they were both quiet. The day was over; neither knew what tomorrow would bring.

They lay together on the grass in the yard, gazing up at the starry sky, tracing constellations for each other, talking about faraway planets and universes, for the questions of their own near world were too weighty to consider. The night turned cool, and they went up to the loft.

Andy reached for her, and she fell willingly into his arms. Except for the warm glow where the dull ache had once resided, she might have thought they had not made love at noon. They seemed that starved for each other. He entered her swiftly, without preliminaries, and they raced to a shattering overwhelming conclusion.

Afterward sleep was elusive. She lay close to him, wondering why their lovemaking had not made her drowsy. The day had been so full. Her eyes should be closing voluntarily, but instead she stared into the darkness, trying to distinguish the shape of the future. But all she could see were shadows.

AT FIRST LIGHT Joy crept downstairs and made coffee. Not long after she heard Andy's bare feet on the stairs. "I didn't mean to wake you," she said.

"I reached over and you weren't there. Are you okay?"

"The question is, are we okay?" She fixed a mug of coffee for him.

"Come up to New Hampshire with me," he urged. "We'll both get some rest, get to know each other again. Think about the future. We've got to think about it sometime."

"I've got to go back to the city. I've got a job, commitments to people."

"And you've got an understudy. What about your commitment to yourself, Joy? When are you going to give that the attention it deserves?"

A sick feeling began to grow in her stomach. "I'm taking care of it. It may not seem that way to you, but I am. I can't run my life the way you run yours, Andy. It won't work."

"From what you told me yesterday the way you're running your life isn't working, either. You could at least free yourself up and think about it."

"And you can stop telling me what to do," she said angrily.

"All right," he said in a strained voice, "but not until I've said one more thing. You came here to me. You said you needed me, wanted me. That has to go further than the bedroom, Joy. You asked me if I wanted you, quirks, faults and all. Now I'm asking you if you want me— quirks, faults, advice and all the rest."

"I want you, Andy. I need you." Her voice quavered, and she took a deep breath. "But I have to live my own life. If I don't have my own life I have nothing to give you."

He looked at her steadily, staring at the rumpled T-shirt of his that she had slept in, her hair mussed, no makeup. She was lovely like this. He wanted to see her this way every morning, but it was impossible if she continued to waste herself and her talent. "I can't stand by and watch you ruin your life. And I don't want to be there only to pick up the pieces." He went to her and held her. "Make a life with me here, Joy. I know I can make you happy."

"I won't hold you responsible for my happiness. That won't do either of us any good." She unfolded his arms from around her and stepped away from him.

"If you won't take love, will you take a job?" he said bitterly.

"I have a job, Andy. I've got to go back and finish it. If I don't I won't be able to live with myself." He started to turn away from her. "Wait, please. I have to tell you one more thing. Without yesterday I wouldn't have been able to. I'll cherish the memory—always." She moved quickly to the bottom of the stairs. "I'll go as soon as I've dressed." She took the stairs two at a time and held her tears until the shower was running full blast.

She was calmer when she had showered and dressed. Downstairs she found Andy standing in front of the fireplace, head hanging loosely, one arm resting on the mantelpiece. "Goodbye," she said quietly.

He straightened and turned to her. "You won't reconsider?"

"We're always going to be running into the same brick wall."

"Unless one of us finds a chink in it."

"I'll call you if I do," she said with a wan smile.

"Will you?"

They gave each other a last long look, as if to memorize the moment. If she could have, Joy would have frozen the scene right there, like you could with a piece of film. But this was life—you couldn't stop the action, or go back. The tape kept running, no matter what. She wrenched her eyes from his and walked away.

"Take care of yourself," he called as she went through the door.

I'll have to, she thought, and quickened her pace.

13

JOY RETURNED TO NEW YORK without the dull ache inside that had plagued her for so many months, but with a sadness that felt like two weights pressing down on her shoulders. That night she sat by her window and reread *Romeo and Juliet*. She wept profusely when she reached the speech of Juliet's that she had recited to Andy the first night they had made love. Only the comfort she took in the beauty of Shakespeare's words allowed her to finish reading the play. When she closed the thick well-thumbed book, she understood as never before the meaning of "star-cross'd lovers."

The next day she reported to rehearsal and sweated through another week of changes, then ten interminable days of previews. Since their first night in Washington, the cast had not done a single show exactly like the previous one. She had long ago stopped believing that anything had continuity. New York was hot and dirty. She lost weight; she felt tired and dragged out a lot of the time.

While Joy was being whittled down by the show, the city and her sadness, Andy was whittling away his days under a large elm behind his friend's theater in New Hampshire. The day he arrived he attended a rehearsal and performance, but he might have been on another planet for all the attention he paid. The next day he took up residence under the tree and read for a couple of hours. After that his book went untouched.

He dozed and dreamed; his most strenuous activity was chewing on a blade or two of the thick grass that grew around the tree. Until he stopped and sat down he hadn't realized how tired he was. Eight years was a long time to go at breakneck speed. He had been running on empty for a long time; his tank needed refilling.

His thoughts turned often to Joy. They were both grown-up, intelligent people. Surely they could find a way to be together without either of them giving up their integrity. *But you'll have to stop trying to run her the way you run the theater,* an inner voice told him. *What's the difference if she goes off to do a show somewhere else for a couple of months? Why is that so threatening?* he asked himself. *If she comes to the Arc,* he argued back, *I'll need her there. There'll be so much to do.* He wouldn't want her gallivanting all over the place, especially if she was going to get involved with shows like the one she was in now. No, she'd have to make a firm commitment to him and to the Arc; they went together.

Then one day a truly shocking thought struck him— he could leave the theater for days, weeks, even a month or two at a time. It wouldn't fall apart without him; it would be there when he returned. And not only when the theater wasn't operating, like now. Next summer he might look for a job in stock, get to spend a few weeks in the country, maybe even the whole season. That would be fun and refreshing. Especially if Joy were there with him.

But, that stickler of an inner voice said, *if she could come with you to summer stock, why shouldn't she go somewhere on her own?* He thought about it for the rest of the day, and on subsequent days, but couldn't come up with a good answer.

THE HEAT WAVE that had a vise grip on New York seemed to make everything move in slow motion. Joy began to think opening night would never arrive. She longed for it; once the critics saw *Three-Ring Circus* the closing notice would surely go up. The producers, no matter how determined and how limitless their funds, could not afford to keep a show open in New York for too long without substantial audiences. They were already way over budget. At some point they would have to cut their losses.

But when the day of the opening arrived, instead of the relief she had anticipated, Joy had an attack of fear and nerves. Nothing helped—not relaxation exercises, a cooling swim, a sauna or a cold shower. The thought of food was nauseating, but she had to eat something. The show was too energetic to risk performing in this heat without some sustenance, even in an air-conditioned theater.

Late in the afternoon she managed to choke down a bowl of fruit salad with yogurt and lay on her bed until it was time to leave for the theater. She tried to figure out what was making her so nervous. She'd performed the show for critics and audiences before and had survived. Why was tonight different? The thought of being an object of ridicule for sharp-tongued New York critics was particularly disturbing. But she had let herself in for it. Her own choices had led her to this point. It wasn't really the critics, she decided after some more thought. A bad review would only sting for a while. What she was afraid of was what would happen tomorrow or next week after the inevitable closing notice was posted. Would she continue to go from one unfulfilling job to the next? That wasn't what she wanted, that wasn't what she had dreamed about for so many years.

Maybe she should go back to Andy, stay at the Arc, not let herself in for any more of the unpleasant tricks the "real world" could play on her. But that would never work. No, she had to learn to trust herself again, to trust her judgment. She had to follow her instincts and not let herself get sidetracked by what other people thought was good for her or by her own denial of reality. She had known that *Three-Ring Circus* wasn't right for her, and yet she had walked right into it. She couldn't do that anymore. A lion tamer didn't stay alive because he pretended the lion had no teeth.

Suddenly she broke out in a cold sweat, and her breathing became rapid and shallow. She stumbled to the bathroom and bathed her face and wrists in cool water. What a time for an anxiety attack, she thought, glancing at the mirror. Her skin was pale, her eyes too bright, every bone prominent. *And I have to go out there and be wacky and funny tonight, bounce on a trampoline and swing on a trapeze?* She sank down onto the edge of the tub. She'd never be able to do it. Never.

Somehow she'd have to, though; it was time to go to the theater. She threw on a pair of shorts and a T-shirt and slipped a dry cleaner's bag over her coolest dress. If the fates were kind she'd only have to go to one party for this show; tonight would take care of both the opening and the closing.

At the theater she signed in and went to her dressing room, changed into her costume and did a series of warm-up exercises, humming to wake up her vocal cords at the same time. Her body and her voice had taken a beating during the grueling out-of-town tryouts. She had bruises up and down her shins from climbing the set's ladders; her vocal cords were tired and irritated and on the verge of hoarseness.

Finally the assistant stage manager called for the first act beginners, and Joy took her place for the opening number, telling herself that once she got onstage everything would be fine. She didn't collapse in the first few seconds, and her voice and moves became more confident as the number progressed. But when she and her partner stepped out of the chorus line for their first duet, she unconsciously slipped into one of the old routines. She didn't realize it until she reached for his hand on a turn and it wasn't there. He was halfway across the stage, doing entirely different steps.

She smiled broadly to cover the panic; she couldn't remember the new steps. All she could remember was snatches of all the routines that had come before. She kept smiling and moving, trying to get to the other side of the stage and pick up the right routine. There were sniggers from the audience, and she looked beseechingly at her partner. He tried to mouth the steps for her inconspicuously, but succeeded only in looking like an amateur ventriloquist. Suddenly the situation struck her as ludicrously funny, and she had to fight the urge to collapse into giggles then and there. She managed to stifle herself until the end of the solo and stepped back with relief into the ranks of the chorus.

"Sorry about that," Joy apologized when they came offstage.

"I went blank for a second myself. If I could have figured out which of the thousands of routines you were doing, I'd have joined you." He put a weary hand to his forehead, shook his head despairingly, then dashed off for his next entrance on the opposite side of the stage.

Joy paced the wings, humming under her breath to keep her vocal cords supple. She had a brief scene next, followed by a scramble up the ladder, a fall into the trampoline and then she went right into a song. She was running through her moves when she noticed something odd about the scene taking place onstage between the leading lady and man. She listened more closely and realized that whole chunks of dialogue were missing; they had gone up on—forgotten—their lines. There were more chuckles from the audience, and the conductor struck up the introduction to their duet. *Holy cow*, she thought to herself. *I'm almost on. If I hadn't been listening I might have missed my cue.* She stood by for the applause after their number that signaled her entrance.

The clapping was brief and weak, and Joy and her partner took the stage. They tossed their lines at each other like hot potatoes, wanting only to get rid of them, and Joy raced up the ladder, scraping her left shin painfully. She winced and dived onto the trampoline, righted herself and somersaulted off it to center stage. Her aching leg threw her timing off, and she missed the first beat of her song. She thought the conductor would vamp until she was ready, but he probably hadn't noticed she was late and went right into the music. She mustered her poise and came in on the second line of the lyric, which didn't make any sense at all without the first line. But she smiled as if it did and sang on.

The throbbing in her shin grew so intense it was hard for her to keep her mind on singing. The only word that wanted to come out of her mouth was a loud, "Ouch!" The lyrics and the shout of pain waged a sparring match inside her head. She tried to deflect her attention by concentrating on the music, but soon discovered that was a bad tactic. The "Ouch" knocked out one of the words of the song and sprang into its place. She was so surprised she flubbed the entire line. Trying not to panic, she glued her eyes to the conductor's baton and used his steady motions to help her back into the song. She finished the number without further incident and slunk gratefully into the wings. *If only I didn't have to go back*, she thought as she listened to the feeble applause.

She iced her shin while waiting for the act's final number, wishing she could sink into the floor and disappear. Anything would be better than going back out there. But when the cue came she went on, like the trouper she was. The act ended, and she collapsed in her dressing room, wondering if it were possible to close a show before the second act.

There was a knock at the door, and she said, "Come in." The door opened slowly, and a sandy head peeked around the edge. "Andy?" she said softly.

"Can I come in?"

"Only if you've got a getaway car waiting in the alley."

"That bad, huh?"

"Worse. Were you in the audience?"

He came into the room and shut the door behind him. "Yeah."

"Then you don't have to ask." Suddenly it hit her that Andy was standing in her dressing room. She had been so numb she hadn't felt the impact. Now she began to thaw, to feel. He had his nerve showing up here now. What right did he have to waltz into her dressing room? "What are you doing here?" she asked warily.

"Offering moral support."

"Did you bring a few truckloads? Since I haven't got any morals to start with I might need a lot."

"I deserve that," he answered quietly. "I was rough on you that morning. I'm sorry."

"So am I," she said, a little less coldly.

He let a few seconds go by and changed the subject. He hadn't fast-talked his way backstage to rehash their old argument. "I didn't know you could sing so well."

"When I remember the words," she said caustically.

"You remembered most of them," he said with a grin. "What happened?" She rolled up the leg of her costume and pointed to the new bruise. He knelt beside her to examine it. "Nasty," he commented.

"The whole show is nasty. You were right. I should've quit."

"No, I wasn't right."

She laughed mirthlessly. "Maybe you weren't, but I still should have quit." She sighed heavily. "Well, it will all be over soon anyway."

"There's still one way out."

"What's that?" she asked skeptically.

"Don't you know the old story?" He stood up and perched on the arm of her chair. "A very famous actress once found herself in an absolute turkey of a show. From the first day it was one disaster after another. But somehow they managed to get to the dress rehearsal. The actress is in the middle of her big monologue and she hears a creak, then a rumble. She looks up and the entire set collapses around her. There is an absolute hush in the theater. Everyone is thinking the worst—that she's badly injured or even dead. Then the debris begins to move. She sticks her head up, takes a beat and then yells, 'Who do I have to sleep with to—'"

"'—get *out* of this show?'" Joy jumped in, finishing the punch line with him. She dissolved in laughter and rested her head on Andy's thigh. Of course she'd heard the story. Everyone in the theater had heard it. She looked up at him to say something but was overtaken by laughter.

"It's good to see you laughing," he said lightly.

"What's so funny, Joy?" Carrie Walton, the leading lady, had stuck her head in the door.

Joy looked up at Carrie with a deadpan expression and said, "Who do I have to sleep with to get—"

"—out of this show?" Carrie echoed with her. She clutched the door as she began to laugh. "How true, how true," she said. Someone else passed by, and Joy and Carrie repeated the line. The laughter attracted others, and soon most of the cast was standing in the corridor outside Joy's dressing room in stitches.

By the time the second act was called, the company was feeling much more relaxed. There wasn't anything they could do to save the show, but they had a lot more fun onstage and the audience response picked up.

"Let's not get too cheerful, chickadees," Carrie warned at the second act curtain. "We wouldn't want to get a good review, would we?"

Heaven forbid, Joy thought as she returned to her dressing room. She touched up her hair and makeup and changed into her third act costume, feeling better, more relaxed than she had in weeks. Andy's surprise appearance had something to do with it, but knowing that her association with *Three-Ring Circus* was almost at an end contributed as well. She thought back to the severe anxiety attack she'd had before the performance. Tomorrow—or next week if the show lasted that long—she'd start looking for work again. But this time she'd be more careful. She wouldn't take a job for the sake of having one; she'd sweat it out on unemployment or go back to waitressing if she had to rather than repeat this experience. The lesson had been an expensive one—her salary from rehearsals and out-of-town tryouts wouldn't begin to pay for all the coaching she'd taken—but she had learned it well.

And there was Andy. He'd come to her this time. He'd said she was right not to quit the show. For a brief moment she let herself hope that they would find a way to be together, but she quickly quashed the glimmering possibility. No, Andy would only end up using her experience as a reason for her to come back to Philadelphia. If she ever went back there they would have to have an understanding that she was free to come and go as she felt she needed to. He would never agree to that.

But he had come to wish her well tonight. That was important, important to how she remembered him and their love and their time together. It lightened the great load of sadness she had carried away with her.

The call came for the third act, and she marched intrepidly to the wings, knowing she would survive the opening and that she would be able to carry on tomorrow or whenever the show closed. The final curtain rang down to mostly polite applause and a few hisses and catcalls. The cast huddled together on the stage, arms draped around one another, holding one another up. They were hot and tired and spent, but they had come through alive, if not entirely unscathed. Besides Joy's throbbing leg, a sprained wrist and a case of incipient laryngitis had been added to the already long list of injuries.

The director approached the group, and they applauded him. He'd been fair and had worked hard. It wasn't his fault that the material had proved so intractable. "Nice work, everyone. We had a shaky start, but you all pulled together and turned in a good professional performance. I'm sorry to announce there won't be another one."

Joy's first impulse was to let out a whoop, and from the looks on a few other faces she wasn't the only one. But she restrained herself and so did the others. No one was surprised; some were disappointed, most were resigned. Murmuring quietly among themselves the members of the cast returned to their respective dressing rooms.

She sat lazily in her chair for a long while. Not for many months had she felt so free and easy. She took her time dressing. Andy would be meeting her at the cast party, but she didn't feel inclined to hurry. There was no reason to rush and every reason to savor the feeling of relief and release that was seeping into her every cell.

No reporters or photographers were massed at the door of the restaurant tonight. The news that there was no good news must have traveled fast, and the hounds had gone sniffing after bigger stories. The atmosphere inside was subdued; people stood in quiet clumps sippping their drinks. There was none of the frenetic buzzing back and forth that had characterized the opening night party for *Sisters and Daughters*.

Joy spotted Andy near the bar. He saw her and motioned that he would meet her. "Champagne seemed too festive for the occasion," he said, offering her a glass of white wine.

"White wine from the white knight, eh?" She took the glass and raised it to him. "Thanks for coming down tonight, Andy."

"I didn't come to rescue you. You didn't need it." He put his hand on the small of her back to steer her toward a quiet corner. Her dress was backless to the waist; her skin warm and soft to the touch. His fingers tingled, and a familiar shudder coursed through him.

"I don't know about that. I was awfully glad to see you. More than I like to admit. Not to mention surprised."

"I was surprised myself. Didn't decide to come until the last moment."

"You're lucky the show was a bomb. You might not have gotten a ticket."

He raised his eyebrows suggestively. "I have my ways."

She looked at him fondly. "You certainly do." Then the impossibility of their situation came home to her. "What are we going to do, Andy?" she asked plaintively. "We're no good together, we're no good apart."

He gave her a squeeze. "A classic case of the catch-22s," he said lightly.

"You sound very jovial about it."

He shrugged amiably. "I thought this was a party. Why don't we save the heavy stuff for another time? You might as well enjoy yourself tonight. You've earned it—and you won't get another chance."

"That's for sure." He was right. They didn't have to dissect their relationship right this minute. She'd expected to be alone at this party, and now Andy was by her side. She was going to enjoy herself, enjoy the moment. "Come on, I'll introduce you to some of the cast. I'm sure you'll get a kick out of Carrie." She tugged at his arm.

He folded her arm through the crook of his. "You did well tonight, Joy. I know you got off to a bad start, but after that you were fine. I was impressed."

"Thanks," she said. She leaned her head briefly on his shoulder. "It was a long haul, but I made it, didn't I?" Now that the initial relief had taken hold she was beginning to feel proud of what she'd accomplished in the past months.

"Yes, you did."

A bubble of hope formed inside her. Sometimes it took a while to work things out; sometimes you had to look back down the road to see how far you'd come. Perhaps she and Andy hadn't arrived at the edge of an unbridgeable chasm; perhaps they could find something—even a slender vine—to swing across it.

They moved into the mainstream of the party and circulated among the groups. The jolliest were Joy's fellow cast members, who were joking about things that had happened on the road trip, things that hadn't seemed funny at the time, but could be laughed at now. A group of financial backers were resignedly cheerful about the unintended tax shelter they had invested in. The collaborators were looking ahead to avoid the same mistakes in their next show.

Joy spotted Duncan, Sondra's assistant, across the room and pulled Andy along to meet him. Duncan gave her an extravagant hug. "The show was a hoot, Joyful! This one'll be engraved in the history books," he exclaimed with delight.

"But can I erase it from my résumé?" Joy asked with a wry look.

"Don't knock it, darling, Broadway is Broadway. And who's this handsome hunk?" He extended his hand to Andy.

She introduced the two men and asked Duncan if Sondra was at the party. Duncan lowered his voice. "No, she dashed off during the second intermission, muttering darkly about calling the coast about something. Too bad, she's missing a fabulous party. But then she'd miss it even if she were here."

He and Joy giggled guiltily. "Aren't we awful?" she said to Andy.

"I don't think so," he answered. "I only met the woman once, but I suspect she's one of those people who's very good at getting what she wants, but very bad at being respected and liked."

"He's not only cute," Duncan commented to Joy, "but perceptive as well. I must dash. A friend of mine is opening at a cabaret in SoHo. Don't miss the buffet, darlings. The food is to die."

Joy and Andy looked over the lavish buffet, but stopped only to take a small plate of finger foods, which they munched as they continued their rounds of the room. The crowd thinned early, and only the cast was left when the newspapers arrived. The show was royally panned by one, but the cast got kudos for its valiant efforts. The leading and featured players, Joy among them, were singled out for service above and beyond the call of duty. A second reviewer spent most of her column space railing against the forces afoot in the theater that allowed a production like this to come to light; she excused the actors from a share in the responsibility on the grounds of the high unemployment in their profession. The third chose to be wittily vicious, and Joy received her first bad notice in a major

New York newspaper. She was glad Andy was standing beside her as it was read aloud by the director.

"'This reviewer cannot fathom what misguided notion induced the excellent young dramatic actress Joy Kingsley to turn her talents to musical comedy. In future she should confine such self-indulgence to appearances in remote summer stock companies. (The more remote the better.) She did, however, inadvertently express the only possible reaction either to watching or appearing in *Three-Ring Circus*. While climbing the absurd set—suitable only for mountain goats—during the first act, she apparently injured herself. She was then required to deliver one of the show's more cloying ballads. The pain, whether from injury or having to sing the insipid song, proved too great, and an operatic "Ouch!" escaped her midsong. This was one of the few truthful and illuminating moments of the evening.'"

The reviewer was entitled to be as scathing as he pleased, but still it hurt Joy to have such things printed about her. She held on to Andy's arm, and he gave her a sympathetic hug. The papers were passed around, and when everyone had tired of reading and dissecting the dismal notices, the party broke up.

Andy and Joy walked slowly toward her apartment building. The temperature had dropped a few degrees, and the streets, if not cool, were no longer stifling. The pavement was piled with mounds of black plastic garbage bags, and the air had the distinctive New York heat wave smell of sunbaked garbage. At the end of the street a sanitation department crew was tossing bags into the maw of a huge compactor truck that roared like a hungry lion as it crushed its kill. They turned onto the avenue where tamer early-morning delivery trucks were bringing newspapers and milk to newsstands or delis.

"I love the city at this hour," Joy said. "It's like a watchful animal, resting but ready to spring into action."

"Yeah," Andy answered. "Tonight I feel the life and the power of it. I wish it were leashed like this more often, though."

"I understand why you don't like it, Andy. There's a lot not to like, but you've got to admit there's no place quite the same." Suddenly she didn't want the night to end. She wanted to show him one of the things she really loved about her city. He had showed her so much of what he loved in Philadelphia. "Want to do something really 'New York'?" she asked eagerly.

"I'm game," he answered.

"Let me buy you breakfast at the Central Diner. I'm starving. I hardly ate anything yesterday."

They walked west, almost to the Hudson, to a district of commercial buildings and warehouses. The diner was on a corner, lit by a blinking pink-and-blue neon sign. It was set back from the street, and the narrow asphalt parking lot in front was packed with taxis and delivery vans, even a police car.

"If we're lucky," Joy said, "we'll get a booth in the front part. That's the most fun." As they walked in the door, two police officers vacated a booth. "It must be our night," she commented as they slid into the red vinyl seats.

"Must be," he agreed, reaching across the table for her hand. He looked around the place. "Phew," he said with a shake of his head, "talk about central casting."

Every type of New Yorker was seated in the diner— uniformed delivery men; cigar-chomping cabbies;

young professionals winding down a night at one of the local discos; tidy surburban salesmen in short-sleeved white shirts and thin ties; a pair of punks visiting from the East Village, eyes shaded by wraparound sunglasses, their basic black and studs livened by a green ponytail for him and an eggplant-purple crew cut for her.

"This is one of the best places in the city to do research for a part," Joy said. "When I was waitressing I used to come here a lot after my shift. To watch people. Good food, too."

They both ordered the breakfast special—eggs and bacon, toast and home fries, juice and coffee—from a waitress in a tight black uniform and frilly apron. She had a hard look—jet black dyed hair, lots of bright blue eye shadow and a turned down red-painted mouth. But when she spoke she had a lilting Irish brogue, the mouth softened, the eyes twinkled.

"She's one of my favorites," Joy whispered when the woman was gone. "Tough on the outside, fluffy on the inside. It's a great choice for building a character—to be something so different than what you appear to be."

"You really love the city, don't you?" Andy said thoughtfully.

"Yes. It's not just the power and the excitement; it's the people. Where else could you find a place like this? So many different types in one place. It's one of the best acting schools in town. You can learn all night for the price of a cup of coffee."

Their waitress returned, dishes stacked on her right arm like planes on a runway. She landed each one safely on their table, told them sweetly to enjoy their meal and went away.

The smoky smell of the bacon went straight to Joy's head. She hadn't had an appetite for weeks and weeks, but now she dug into her food.

"Boy, oh boy," Andy said with a short laugh. "You come in here and not only do you look at the truck drivers, you start eating like one."

She swallowed a big bite of toast. "Eat," she told him, "Cold eggs are lousy."

They enjoyed their food and lingered over coffee, watching the free floor show put on by the waitresses, short-order cooks, the mountainous woman behind the cash register and the ever-changing parade of characters. But even the coffee couldn't stifle the yawns brought on by tiredness and the full meal. They left the diner and headed east. The street was like a tunnel between the buildings, and at the other end—with the sparse traffic they could see clear across the island—the sky was turning pink over the East River.

Andy draped his arm around her shoulder and held her tight. "It looks rosy over there," he said, "like a new day should."

"It is a new day, Andy," she said fervently, and wrapped her arms around his waist.

They stood on the pavement, holding each other and watching the sky. The dawn brightened quickly, the rosy glow turning to pale yellow. They walked on, losing sight of the eastern sky as they turned onto Ninth Avenue, but by then they had eyes only for each other.

In her apartment Joy lowered the blinds to keep the sun and the heat out. They undressed and climbed into her bed together, kissing and clinging to each other. They made love slowly and tenderly, without the urgency that usually overtook them as soon as they began to touch. The music she and Andy played together took on rich rumbling overtones that resonated throughout their bodies. The vibrant new chords seemed to spill over into the room, a lush accompaniment to their ecstasy. They sustained the highest notes of their song for an eternity and finished with a gentle coda that lulled them into deep sleep.

14

A SHRILL RINGING was the next sound Joy heard. She was so lost in sleep that she began to grope for her alarm clock, then realized it was the phone she was hearing. She stumbled to her desk. "'Lo?" she said hoarsely.

"I thought you'd be awake by now," Sondra said gruffly without preliminaries or apology.

"I was out late," Joy mumbled. She could hardly open her eyes or keep from being dragged down into sleep while standing up.

"It doesn't matter. You can sleep on the plane."

"What plane?" Joy asked groggily.

"The plane to L.A. You need to get out of town for a while. In a couple of months no one will remember there even was a show called *Three-Ring Circus*, much less that you were in it."

Joy shook herself awake. Sondra's steely voice meant she wasn't kidding. "I don't want to go to L.A.," she said.

"Of course you do. There's a new sitcom casting, and as soon as somebody wakes up out there I'll be getting you an audition. And there are zillions of film and TV people you'll want to see. There's even some decent theater out there these days, but—"

"I don't think you heard me, Sondra. I don't want to go to L.A.," Joy said firmly. She was wide awake now and starting to seethe.

"Joy, you are persona non grata in this town. Plus you owe me several thousand dollars. I don't intend to wait around for it until things simmer down."

"So send me up for some commercials or a soap opera. Here. I have no intention of running off to California."

"If you intend to have an agent, you'd better start packing your suitcase."

Hold on, Joy said to herself. Sondra had no right to play the mistress of the manor and treat her like an indiscreet parlor maid who had to be banished to a country cottage. "I let you railroad me once, Sondra. I'm not going to let you do it again."

"I busted my butt to get you that job, and this is the thanks I get?" Sondra raged.

As if I didn't bust my butt, Joy thought angrily, *not to mention my shins*. She wanted to lash out, but she forced herself to control her temper and maintain a professional attitude. "I appreciate your efforts, Sondra, but I won't take any more jobs just for the sake of having one. And I won't be badgered any more. You seem to have forgotten, but I don't work for you, you work for me."

"If you're not on that plane tonight, Joy, you won't work for anyone, not for a long time!"

Joy held on to the edge of her desk and took a deep breath. "Not only will I not be dictated to, Sondra, I will not be threatened. I want to terminate our agreement."

"Fine. You'll hear from my lawyer. And I meant what I said. It will be a long time before you work again in this town." She slammed down the phone hard.

Shaking with rage, Joy replaced the phone in its cradle. She turned to see Andy with his arms propped under his head, grinning lazily. "It's not funny. I just fired my agent," she said fiercely, "and she promised to blacklist me."

"So I gathered."

"It's just what you wanted to hear, isn't it?" she stormed. "Another I-told-you-so to fling in my face. I suppose you'll expect me to come running back to Philadelphia now?"

"Not necessarily. But the offer still stands."

"Oooooh," Joy growled. "How can you lie there so calmly?"

"Is it going to do any good if I get upset? Maybe you ought to beat on the bed or throw a pillow around. It might make you feel better."

"Dr. Thornhill's cure for disaster. Unconditionally guaranteed, no doubt."

He tossed a pillow at her. "Try it out. No charge for the first treatment."

She heaved the pillow back at him with all her might, and he took the soft blow full in the face without trying to defend himself. She hated to admit it, but she did feel better after catapulting some of her anger with the pillow. "How much does it cost for a second go?" she asked sheepishly.

He considered. "Two hugs and a kiss. No make that two kisses."

"You drive a hard bargain, buster." She took up the pillow again and lobbed it at him. This time he caught it and took it in his arms. He squeezed it tight and brought it to his lips. "Wait a minute," she said with a giggle. "I didn't think you were going to take it out on the pillow. I thought I was the one who had to pay up."

"No, no," he said, grimacing. "I wouldn't want to hug and kiss you."

"You wouldn't, would you?" She snatched the pillow from him and hopped onto the bed. "No one will ever say that Joy Kingsley doesn't pay her debts." She threw her arms around him and bussed him soundly on the mouth. "One hug, one kiss. I owe you one more." She repeated the routine and lay back in his arms. After a while she said, "I've really done it now. Cooked my goose but good."

"I wouldn't take Sondra Carroll too seriously. Her bark is probably worse than her bite."

"Her bark's bad enough," she commented dryly.

"She might give you a hard time, Joy, but she can't ruin you. Only you can do that."

"Do you really think so?" she asked doubtfully. "Or are you saying that to make me feel better?"

"You're very talented. And spunky to boot. You'll come through this."

"Thanks," she said. "You're a real friend." Whatever happened between them in the future, she knew she could count on his friendship and support from now on.

"I'm more than your friend, Joy." He kissed her forehead and smoothed her hair back from her face. "The offer still stands. I'd be happy to have you at the Arc," he said quietly.

It would be so easy to go back now, to leave the mess she'd made for herself behind. "Is there something you'd like me to audition for?" Maybe it would be a good idea to get out of town until the storm clouds blew over, she thought.

"There isn't anything for you to audition for now. But there's plenty to do. The play contest and—"

"I can't, Andy. Don't try to tempt me. I've gotten myself into this. I'll have to get myself out."

"And after that?"

"I don't know," she said honestly. "We'll see."

He hid his disappointment and embraced her. "You know where I am if you need me."

She burrowed her face in his warm chest. Letting him leave her would be hard. She didn't want to do it, but she knew she could never look herself in the mirror again if she ran off to an easy refuge in Philadelphia, no matter how strong her feelings for him were.

"I've got to get going, Joy," he said gently, and lifted her head from his chest.

"So soon?"

"I've got a lunch date at one."

"You'll never get back to Philadelphia in twenty minutes."

He ruffled her hair. "It's here in the city, silly. I'm getting together with a couple of pals from graduate school."

"Oh," she said with surprise. Andy never wanted to stay in New York any longer than was absolutely necessary. "I thought you only decided to come up on the spur of the moment."

"I did. I called them when I got in last night. Decided it would be good to see what they're up to, maybe kick around a few ideas."

"Who are you seeing? And what sort of ideas?"

He named the heads of two prominent off-Broadway producing organizations. "If that's okay with you, Miss Nosey Parker." He sat up and swung his legs over the edge of the bed. He didn't say anything further; the meeting might not come to anything. "I've got to shower. I don't want to be too late."

Joy snuggled down into the bed. She didn't want to get up; she didn't want him to go. She didn't want to face what had to be faced. Would it have turned out differently if Andy hadn't shown up last night? Would she have come to the same conclusions on her own? Would she have had the nerve to fire Sondra? She liked to think she would have, but she would never be certain. And what if she'd told him to get lost? What would have happened then? He emerged from the bathroom, freshly shaved, curls still damp. "What would you have done if you hadn't stayed with me last night?" she asked.

"New York's full of hotels," he answered.

"Would you have stayed over for your lunch date or gone back last night?" He'd glided over her questions before, and she was more than normally curious about what Andy might have to discuss with the people he had mentioned.

"Maybe, maybe not. What's with all the questions?" He sat on the edge of the bed, picked up her hand and kissed it.

"Just my overactive brain trying to postpone the inevitable, I guess."

"And what's that?"

"Getting up, for one thing."

He leaned in close and kissed her tenderly. "You'll be fine." He kissed her again and started to pull away. She clung to him.

"When will I see you?" she whispered.

"I don't know, Joy. We both have things to work out. Let's just say that the phone lines are open."

"And the heart lines?"

"And the heart lines," he confirmed. He kissed her once more and was gone.

The door clicked shut, and for one awful moment Joy buried her head under a pillow, certain that she never wanted to come out, certain that she would not survive if she did. But the terrible paralyzing feeling passed, and she got out of bed. The floor felt shaky under her feet as she took her first steps, but she moved carefully into the kitchen and put on the coffee.

Performing the simple task gave her the impetus to go on, and she picked up the phone and put in a call to Attorneys for the Arts, a group of volunteer lawyers who made themselves available in predicaments such as hers. She outlined her problem and was given an appointment for later that afternoon. That done she pulled out a pad and pencil and began to think about what she should do next.

ANDY STAYED ON in the restaurant after his friends had rushed back to their offices, sipping a second cappuccino. His idea for setting up an exchange program between theirs and other New York groups and regional theaters all over the country had gone over well. They'd brainstormed about it and had drawn up lists of people each of them would contact. With all of them so busy, it could take a year or more to get the plan off the ground, but he was excited and optimistic about its eventual success.

Sitting under that elm in New Hampshire he'd thought a lot about some of the things Joy had said to him. He *had* become isolated, too comfortable being the biggest fish in the small pond he'd dug out for himself. But he also knew he couldn't involve himself in the part of the theater world that operated principally for profit. He'd thought long and hard about an alternative, mindful for once of his personal needs as well as his professional ones.

Joy would never be happy staying exclusively in Philadelphia, but with this plan in operation it would be possible for her, for both of them in fact, to divide their time, to serve both their needs without killing their love. She would see he was serious about finding a way for them to stay together, a way for him to expand the scope of his work without compromising his values. Of course the whole thing could backfire; she could still refuse to marry him. But he would put every ounce of effort into seeing that she didn't.

There was only one problem—how to get her back at the Arc in the first place and unfold his plan. He drained his coffee and left the table. He could think about that on the way home.

15

THE NEXT TWO WEEKS were painful and difficult for Joy. With the help of her volunteer attorney, she worked out an agreement with Sondra to repay the money she owed for her lessons and coaching sessions. The only problem was where to get the money. She had some savings, but she would need that to tide her over until her next job. She was eligible for unemployment compensation, but the check wouldn't go far, and she refused to go back to waiting tables until she had exhausted all other possibilities.

She found that getting appointments to see other agents was relatively easy, now that she had some Broadway credits. But once they heard she had been one of Sondra Carroll's clients, interest flagged visibly. She was determined not to fall into the same trap she had fallen into with Sondra and was honest with the other agents about the reason for the breakup. But only a handful—mostly young agents with little power and little to lose—ever called her a second time, and she could count the auditions her efforts had produced on one hand.

The contacts that she had made through Sondra were almost impossible to maintain. Several people were downright rude when she phoned, others cold, some cool and noncommittal. A few were straight with her— they'd been told by Sondra that she was unreliable and unprofessional. They listened to her side of the story—but they'd been dealing with Sondra for years, and they barely knew Joy. She had to face facts—the strikes Sondra had hurled at her were threatening to put her out of the ball game altogether.

So she turned her attention to paying the rent and began making the rounds of people who cast television and radio commercials and hired models for print advertising. Sondra's clients rarely had to sell dog food or floor wax to make ends meet. But even in this area Joy found that an undeserved reputation preceded her. She would have thought that it was in Sondra's interest to let her earn the money to pay her off. But she suspected Sondra didn't really care that much about the money. *I assaulted her ego*, it occurred to Joy, *so I'm being punished.* In desperation she phoned Duncan at home one evening and asked him to have lunch with her the next day.

"Not unless I can wear a paper bag over my head. If Sondra hears we were seen together, it'll mean my job. But I can meet you at your apartment later on. I know tons of people in your building. No one has to know I'm coming to see you."

He arrived at her door that evening with a large bouquet. "They're beautiful," she exclaimed. "How sweet of you." She kissed him on the cheek and ushered him into the apartment.

"It was the least I could do. I took the money out of petty cash," he told her brazenly. "You deserve more, but there was only $9.63 in the kitty. Sondra not only has the manners of a warthog, she's cheap." He sat down on the couch and crossed his legs, careful not to disturb the sharp crease of his trousers.

"Then why do you work for her?" she called from the kitchen as she ran water into a vase for the flowers.

"For the same reason you signed with her; she's one of the best in the business. I've never seen her like this, though, Joyful. She's been screaming the blue meanies. What did you say to her?" Joy repeated the conversation. "That's it?" he asked incredulously.

"Why does she have it in for me?" Joy asked him. She put the flowers on the coffee table and sat down beside him.

"I'm not sure, but I think she had really big plans for you. And she knew she'd made a big mistake with *Three-Ring Circus*. If there's one thing Sondra doesn't like, it's to be told she's wrong—especially when it's true. She's overcompensating."

"That's the understatement of the year."

"She'll get over it. She can't go on like this forever. It's taking up too much of her time."

"That's a small comfort. What do I do in the meantime?"

"I've been thinking of opening my own office. Want to be my first client?"

"And your last?"

"I see your point," he said dryly. "I don't know if there's anything you *can* do. I've tried to smooth things over some on my end, but it's not easy. I know you're going to think this is the chicken way out, but why don't you get out of town for a while? You and Andy what's-his-face seemed to be thick as thieves at the party after the circus folded. Can't he dig up something for you?"

"He'd be only too willing. That's the problem," she replied.

"Too many strings attached, eh?"

She nodded silently.

After Duncan left she thought yet again about calling Andy, but couldn't do it. Running back to the Arc would be like running home to your mother after a bully hit you in the school yard. She wasn't a child in need of protection anymore.

The next day she woke up filled with fresh resolve. She signed up for a Shakespeare workshop, volunteered at the Playwright's Guild to participate in readings of new plays, went over to the union office to check the call-board and dropped in on a few open interviews that sounded interesting. Everyone knew the shows were mostly cast by the time they held the open interviews that the union required, but still it gave her the feeling of doing something constructive. In the afternoon she made a few calls on casting directors who worked in commercials and withdrew some money from the bank to pay for the new batch of pictures and résumés she'd had printed. She'd see this through no matter what it took.

The following week she got her first break—a print ad for a local bank. The fee for the shoot was modest, but at least she had gotten some work for herself. True, it was far from getting a part in a play and well removed from Sondra's sphere of influence, but psychologically it meant a great deal to her. She decided to concentrate her efforts on commercials for the next couple of weeks and then test the theatrical currents again to see if Sondra's deadly undertow had ebbed.

She kept busy and kept her spirits up; she exercised vigorously every day and spent a lot of time catching up with friends. She bought the trade papers and called around to directors she'd worked with in off-off-Broadway showcase productions. Showcases didn't pay anything, but they offered an opportunity to work on a role and present it to an audience.

But there came a time every day when she had to return to her empty apartment and face a night alone. Her thoughts inevitably turned to Andy—how comforting it would be to have his arms around her, to wake up with him in the morning. In Philadelphia she had loved sharing the simple things with him, almost as much as the work, maybe even more than the work. It was hard to tell anymore; it seemed so long ago. Every night, as she carefully planned the next day, finding activities to fill each waking moment, she remembered the months at the Arc when she had had more things to do than minutes to do them.

After several auditions, she was offered and accepted a small part in a showcase production of a new comedy. It wasn't much, but she had gotten it all on her own. By her own diligent efforts she'd begun to pull herself up out of the depths. Each day she felt a little stronger, a little better about herself.

Still, Andy stayed on her mind. She'd picked herself up and dusted herself off, as she'd needed to do. But wasn't she being just as stubborn in her own way as Andy had been in his, perhaps even more so? The last time she'd seen him he hadn't been as rigid and demanding as he had been when she had left the Arc back in March. He had come to her here in the city, taken time the next day to see some colleagues and left the Arc entirely to go to New Hampshire. Perhaps he was changing while she was staying tied to old dreams, old needs. She found herself moving closer and closer to picking up the phone.

Andy beat her to it. When she returned from her Shakespeare workshop one day, there was a message on her answering service to call the Arc Theater regarding an audition. The message wasn't from Andy himself, but from someone called Jeff Stone. She wondered who he was as she dialed the number. He identified himself as the new stage manager and asked her if she was available to audition for the role of Carol in Tennessee Williams's *Orpheus Descending*.

"I didn't know that was on the schedule for this season," she said, somewhat surprised.

"There was a change just before I started work here last week. I believe there was some trouble with the rights on the other play Andy had scheduled."

"I see," she said. She had once told Andy she would love to play this role. The movie version with Joanne Woodward and Marlon Brando was one of her all-time favorites.

"Are you available Thursday afternoon? I have openings at three-thirty and four-thirty," Jeff Stone was saying. She chose the later slot. "Andy would like you to prepare the two exchanges between Val and Carol in act one, scene one. I know I don't have to give you directions to get here. I've seen the stills from *Sisters and Daughters*, Miss Kingsley. Everyone says it was terrific. I'm looking forward to meeting you."

"Thank you. I'm looking forward to meeting you, too." She double-checked the day and time and the scenes she was to prepare and was about to hang up when she thought to ask, "Can you tell me what's happened to Gretchen, please? Is she still working there?"

There was a small pause before he answered. "She's taken another job—in Seattle."

"That's quite a switch," she said. They exchanged a few more pleasantries and rang off. Something was afoot at the Arc—Gretchen gone, a sudden change in

the schedule to a play she had once expressed an interest in. Andy would have to notify all his subscribers,
allow them refunds if they didn't like the new play,
change his advertising and promotion. All that would
cost time as well as money. Even though it might have
been necessary because of a withdrawal of performing
rights, he wouldn't have undertaken such a decision
lightly. And he might easily have chosen as a replacement a less difficult play to produce than *Orpheus Descending*.

Whatever the reason—and she would have to wait
until she got there to find out—she had been called for
an audition, and she was going to make the most of this
stroke of good fortune. She went to the bookcase for
her copy of the script, grabbed a pad and pencil and sat
down to read.

THE JOURNEY ON THURSDAY seemed as slow as if she
were going by horse and carriage. She was impatient
to get to Philadelphia and wanted to be whisked there
instantly, the way Scotty beamed Captain Kirk and Mr.
Spock on and off the Starship Enterprise. But the train
trundled along at an earthly speed and made four stops
before finally pulling into the Thirtieth Street Station.

Memories flooded back as she rode the escalator up
to the main floor of the station—heartwarming
thoughts of the day she arrived for her first audition and
saying goodbye to Andy here later that night; heart-
rending thoughts of stealing away to audition for Josh
Phillips, of leaving after her terrible row with Andy
over taking the Broadway job, of leaving again when
she came to see him after the road tour.

What would happen now? Would Andy be all business? Was this an audition only for the role, or for

something more? She hurried out the west doors to the taxi stand, eager to get to the theater, to see Andy, to read for the part. After running so hard in New York just to keep from losing ground, the sense of forward motion she felt was compelling, propelling.

The taxi pulled up in front of the Arc, and she stepped out into the bright sunshine. Indian summer was at its height—the air was still warm but with a hint of the nip it would soon have, and in the deep green leaves of the trees it was possible to imagine the first sparks of the fiery colors that would soon burn in them. Like the weather, she was on the verge of enormous changes. She opened the door and entered the theater.

The first thing she saw in the lobby was a picture of herself from *Sisters and Daughters*. *I'm part of this place*, she thought. *And no matter where I go, no matter what else I do, this place is part of me*. That notion made her feel solemn, blessed; performing here had been a ritual that gave her a tie to the place that could never be broken. Being here again could only strengthen that tie—and others she had begun here, ones that could be knotted tighter, more intricately.

The door to the theater opened, and a dark, wiry fellow stepped out to greet her. She saw immediately that Jeff Stone was tuned to the same energy frequency as Andy. With the two of them operating at the same time, she thought, the radio waves from this place could reach the far corners of the solar system.

In the darkened theater she picked out Andy's outline even before her eyes adjusted to the dim light. He was standing directly in front of her in the aisle. She hurried to him, and he took her two hands in his.

"Hello, Joy," he said softly.

"Hello," she whispered, so overcome by the welcoming light in his eyes she could hardly speak.

He let go of her hands and stood back, drinking in the sight of her. "You look better every time I see you."

"So do you." They were both conscious that another person was in the room and chose words that could be taken as an innocent exchange between people who had once worked together. But the small physical space between them was so charged that they came close to disclosing one of nature's deepest secrets. Had they stayed this close for much longer they might have been able to show the world what electricity looked like.

Andy moved away slightly and said, "There's nothing more I need to know about you, so shall we start the reading?"

Joy knew he wasn't talking about what was on her résumé, but what was in her heart. She nodded and pulled her script out of her oversized purse.

He took a seat in the audience, and Jeff followed Joy onto the stage. The very boards felt familiar under her feet, and she went unerringly to the spot where she would get the best glow from the work lights.

"Bottom of page thirteen, please," Andy said.

She turned to the correct page, closed her eyes for a moment, recalled her preparations and began to read. Only when she finished the scene did she realize she had completely forgotten to be nervous—about the audition

16

JOY AND ANDY WALKED OUT the back door of the the-ater and crossed the yard. "I'd like to offer you the part," he said. "Do you want it?"

"I want the role, not charity," she replied, tamping down her excitement.

"The Arc may be a nonprofit organization, but we still have to please our public," he said with a grin. "If I didn't think you could do it, I wouldn't offer it to you, no matter what." She started to say something, but he overrode her. "I didn't audition other people as a mat-ter of form, Joy. I was looking for the best actress. I hoped it would be you, and it was."

"Then I accept," she said. She felt dizzy, stopped walking and closed her eyes for a second.

"What's the matter?" he asked with concern.

She was on the verge of tears. "I was so afraid," she whispered. "I know it's silly, but I was afraid I would never work in the theater again. I didn't even let myself know it until just now. What if I wasn't the best, Andy?"

"Then I would've had a moral dilemma." He put his arm around her waist and guided her forward. "Come inside, Joy. There's so much we need to talk about."

"Yes," she agreed readily.

He offered her a seat on the sofa and stood by the fireplace with his hand resting on the mantel. "I've got a whole speech prepared. Shall I deliver it?"

"Go ahead. I'm feeling speechless myself right now."

"You better settle in. This may take a while."

"Okay." She kicked off her shoes and curled her feet under her.

Andy tapped his fingers nervously on the mantel. He didn't especially like making speeches, but there were so many things that had to be said. "I started to fall in love with you that first day in New York." He gave a self-deprecating laugh. "Talk about not telling yourself stuff—I'd never have invited you out to dinner if I hadn't been more than casually interested. That day you came down here to audition finished me off. I knew I wanted you and I went after you, the way I go after everything. The only trouble was that you had your own ideas about how your life should proceed—as well you should."

He paced for a moment to dissipate some of the edginess he was feeling and then sat next to her on the couch. He needed to be close to her now that he had gotten to the hardest part of what he had to say. "I've never told you this before, Joy, but something like this happened to me once before. A few years ago I fell in love with someone, tried to run her life the way I ran the theater and lost her. I thought I had learned my lesson. I thought wrong. I tried to do it again with you. Fortunately, you wouldn't let me."

"Andy," she interrupted, "you aren't the only one who's made mistakes in this relationship."

"I didn't say I was, but I've thought this through, Joy. I want you to hear it from start to finish. Please."

She touched his hand lightly. "All right, as long as I get my turn later."

"You will," he assured her. "When you left, I tried to throw myself back into my work as if you'd never existed. I didn't do too badly until I had to come up to New York for the opening of *Sisters and Daughters*. When you showed up here that Sunday, I still thought I could convince you to play out the scene the way I had written it, but you left me again. Later on I saw that it took courage for you to do that. It started me thinking. There had to be some way for us to be together that wouldn't involve compromising ourselves. I knew neither of us could do that."

"What about the change in the schedule, Andy? Jeff said there was a problem with rights. It's awfully late for something like that to have happened."

"The change in the schedule was just one of those things. A conflict did come up with a film producer who had optioned the play. I might have fought harder to keep the rights, but I saw an opportunity to approach you, so I took it. It wasn't an easy decision to make, but as soon as you walked into the theater this afternoon I knew it was the right one."

She stretched her legs out on the sofa and he laid a hand on her shin. The gesture was intimate, not provocative, but still it sent a chill through her. The closeness, the way they were talking—and listening—to each other was thrilling. "And I knew I'd been right to come the minute I stepped into the lobby."

"There's only one thing I regret," he continued. "I lost Gretchen over it."

"I'm sorry. I know how much she did to keep the Arc running smoothly."

"It had to come, Joy. It's my own fault. After you left I spent too much time with her. I knew what was happening, but I didn't do anything about it. I was selfish. She had been looking for another job for a while. She told me when she finally quit. But when I wouldn't put up a strong fight with the film producer, she felt she had to go. I had asked her to research the rights on replacement plays, and it didn't take much to see that they all had a good part for you. I'm sorry to lose her, but sometimes other things are more important."

She reached for his hand and squeezed his fingers. "I'm learning about priorities, too," she said.

"For once the theater was less important than finding a way to be with you—forever. I love you, Joy. I want to marry you. Of course I'd like you to work here at the Arc with me, but you don't have to. You can work anywhere, do anything you want or need to do."

"What I need to do right now," she said quietly, "is kiss you." He held out his arms, and she went to him. She touched her lips lightly, sweetly, to his, then cradled his head against her pounding heart. "No matter where I go for a few weeks my heart and soul will be here with you, my love. If I can ever bring myself to leave you, that is."

He tightened his embrace, crushing her soft breasts against his face. "You will—that is if I have anything to say about it."

She kissed the top of his head. "What's going on here? First you ask me to marry you, then you tell me I have to go away."

He pulled away from her and cupped her face with his hands. "I'm the one who should be told what's going on, woman. I've issued a bona fide proposal of marriage and I haven't had a straight answer yet."

"Yes," she said. "Is that straight enough for you?"

"It'll do." He brought his lips down on hers and kissed her fervently. "It will do quite nicely," he murmured. He kissed her again and leaned back in the corner of the couch.

She snuggled against him, dazed, completely content. "You don't really want me to go anywhere, do you?" she purred.

"No, but you may have to."

"Why?"

Briefly he explained his idea for the exchange program.

"What a wonderful idea!" she exclaimed enthusiastically, and asked him several questions about the program.

"Do you think we could discuss this another time?" he asked with amusement. They had been talking for quite a while now, and another priority was presenting itself with increasing insistence. "Wouldn't you rather talk about being engaged or, better yet, seal the bargain?" He reached out to caress a breast and felt the nipple stir through her blouse.

She pushed his hand away playfully. "We can do *that* for the rest of our lives," she said. "And I have a few things I need to say to you, Andy. After all, you've been doing most of the talking."

He nibbled on her earlobe. "We have the rest of our lives to talk," he protested.

Despite the shivery thrills chasing through her, she pushed him away and sat up straighter. "I didn't know what to expect when I came here today. But I was prepared to stay—if you would have me—either to work or for something more. I remember one of the first things you told me, Andy. That I wasn't selective enough about my jobs, that I took anything that came along." She touched his cheek to tell him how important his input was to her. "I was right to go to New York with *Sisters and Daughters*. I needed that experience. But then Sondra came along. I didn't even go to see one other agent. I simply took her offer. Then *Three-Ring Circus* happened by and I took that, too. I hopped right on the train without knowing where it was going. Well, I don't want to do that anymore. I want to know where I'm headed from now on and be sure I want to end up there if I go."

"Do you know where you're going with me, Joy?"

"Yes. I've chosen you. I could have stayed in New York. I could have said no to your proposal. But I'm sure I want to marry you. I'm sure I love you. I've been certain of that for a while. But I wasn't certain that I could live with you if we were always in a tug-of-war about whether I stayed at the Arc or went off to do other work. But now that I know I can leave if I want to, I don't feel I need to." She leaned forward and put a hand on his knee. "I'm not saying I won't or I will, I don't know what will happen. But I feel free, tied to you more tightly than ever before, but freer at the same time. It's ironic, but there it is. I don't know where we'll end up—"

He put an index finger over her lips. "I know where I'd like us to end up now." He raised his eyes and nodded toward the loft, then started to lift her up.

She bore down with her weight to stop him. "Do you understand me, Andy? I need to know."

"I do, my joy. Come upstairs with me. Let me show you just how much I do understand. Please."

She threw her arms around his neck and let herself be whisked up the stairs. When he put her on the bed, she drew him down beside her. Her fingers went eagerly to the buttons on his shirt. He slid his arms under hers and began to undo her blouse.

They undressed each other quickly, anxious to strip away the last barriers between them, to expose their bodies as they had exposed their minds and hearts, to show they were hiding nothing from each other.

"You're so beautiful," Andy whispered huskily.

He cupped each full breast reverently, then ran his hands down the sides of her body, past her buttocks, over her thighs and down to her feet. He bent to her and buried his face in her belly, as if trying to kiss the exact center of her. She stroked his hair and reveled in his touch. Now that they were truly together their lovemaking excited her and promised to fulfill her more than ever before. He rose and straddled her, bent again and took her right nipple in his mouth. Greedily he pulled and suckled at it until she gave out delighted gasps. He teased the other breast the same way until she was panting and weak with wanting him.

He gently coaxed her on top of him, and they came together in one smooth, fluid motion. "You feel so good, so warm," he whispered.

She wrapped her arms tighter around his back and clung to him. She wanted to open up fully to him, wanted him to touch her core, wanted to unlock all her secret places for him. "I can't give you enough. I can't get enough of you," she told him.

"Yes, you can," he answered, moving deeper inside her. "You can have all of me."

With each movement she was filled with larger and larger jolts of electricity. The currents traveled outward through her body, charging each cell, reaching to the ends of her fingers, her toes, taking on added voltage until she was almost unbearably charged. She moved hard and fast against him until each circuit in her body threatened to overload.

Then suddenly it was as if someone had pulled a giant switch. They both stiffened, and a shocking wave of ecstasy was unleased, first in her, then in Andy. She felt as if she were filled with a white light so strong it left her phosphorescent, glowing in the early-evening dusk with a light as strong as the love she felt for him. Gradually she relaxed and snuggled against him, enjoying the state of deep satisfaction and fulfillment she was in. She sighed contentedly and kissed him lovingly.

"Was that enough, my joy?" he asked quietly.

"For now," she said with another contented sigh.

He laughed lightly. "Greedy little thing, aren't you?"

"Not really. Why settle for less when you can have the best? Can I really have this for the rest of my life?" she asked wonderingly.

"I've heard it gets better."

"Impossible," she said, and kissed him again. "I love you so much."

"And I love you," he said, stroking her hair and planting a bumper crop of kisses all over her face.

Dusk turned to night, and they lay in each other's arms, planning their future in soft excited whispers. There were so many things to talk about—when they would marry and where, what sort of wedding they would have, how they could fix up the carriage house to accommodate two, or perhaps more.

Night settled upon them, and they were content to wrap its comforting cloak around them, needing no light to see each other clearly. Juliet's beautiful words, the ones she had recited to Andy the first time they had lain in the hush of night together, came flying into Joy's mind. She took his hand, placed it over her heart and said the words to him again, her voice fraught with meaning and emotion, her eyes misting with tears of happiness.

She told him about reading the play the day she'd left Philadelphia to return to New York for the opening of *Three-Ring Circus*, when it seemed as if they would never be able to find a way to be together. "How I despaired that day, but we're here together now." Her voice was rife with relief, with thankfulness. "Unlike Juliet, I woke up in time. We've saved our love, Andy. We have our happy ending."

"No, my joy, my love, my life," he said, taking her into his arms. "We have our happy beginning."

"Our very happy beginning," she echoed, and raised her face to accept his tender kiss.

Harlequin "Super Celebration"
SWEEPSTAKES

NEW PRIZES—NEW PRIZE FEATURES & CHOICES—MONTHLY

1. To enter the sweepstakes, follow the instructions outlined on the Center Insert Card. Alternate means of entry, NO PURCHASE NECESSARY, you may also enter by mailing your name, address and birthday on a plain 3" x 5" piece of paper to: In U.S.A.: Harlequin "Super Celebration" Sweepstakes, P.O. Box 1867, Buffalo, N.Y. 14240-1867. In Canada: Harlequin "Super Celebration" Sweepstakes, P.O. Box 2800, 5170 Yonge Street, Postal Station A, Willowdale, Ontario M2N 6J3.

2. Winners will be selected in random drawings from all entries received. All prizes will be awarded. These prizes are in addition to any free gifts which might be offered. Versions of this sweepstakes with different prizes may appear in other presentations by TorStar and their affiliates. The maximum value of the prizes offered is $8,000.00. Winners selected will receive the prize offered from their prize package.

3. The selection of winners will be conducted under the supervision of Marden-Kane, an independent judging organization. By entering the sweepstakes, each entrant accepts and agrees to be bound by these rules and the decision of the judges which shall be final and binding. Odds of winning are dependent upon the total number of entries received. Taxes, if any, are the sole responsibility of the winners. Prizes are not transferable. This sweepstakes is scheduled to appear in Retail Outlets of Harlequin Books during the period of June 1986 to December 1986. All entries must be received by January 31st, 1987. The drawing will take place on or about March 1st, 1987 at the offices of Marden-Kane, Lake Success, New York. For Quebec (Canada) residents, any litigation regarding the running of this sweepstakes and the awarding of prizes must be submitted to La Regie de Lotteries et Course du Quebec.

4. This presentation offers the prizes as illustrated on the Center Insert Card.

5. This offer is open to residents of the U.S., and Canada, 18 years or older, except employees of TorStar, its affilliates, subsidiaries, Marden-Kane and all other agencies and persons connected with conducting this sweepstakes. All Federal, State and local laws apply. Void where prohibited or restricted by law. Winners will be notified by mail and may be required to execute an affidavit of eligibility and release which must be returned within 14 days after notification. Winners consent to the use of their name, photograph and/or likeness for advertising and publicity in conjunction with this and similar promotions without additional compensation. One prize per family or household. Canadian winners will be required to answer a skill testing question.

6. For a list of our most recent prize winners, send a stamped, self-addressed envelope to: WINNERS LIST, c/o Marden-Kane, P.O. Box 525, Sayreville, NJ 08872.

No Lucky Number needed to win!

Take 4 books & a surprise gift FREE

SPECIAL LIMITED-TIME OFFER

Mail to **Harlequin Reader Service**®

In the U.S.	In Canada
901 Fuhrmann Blvd.	P.O. Box 2800, Station "A"
P.O. Box 1394	5170 Yonge Street
Buffalo, N.Y. 14240-1394	Willowdale, Ontario M2N 6J3

YES! Please send me 4 free Harlequin Temptation® novels and my free surprise gift. Then send me 4 brand-new novels every month as they come off the presses. Bill me at the low price of $1.99 each — a 13% saving off the retail price. There are no shipping, handling or other hidden costs. There is no minimum number of books I must purchase. I can always return a shipment and cancel at any time. Even if I never buy another book from Harlequin, the 4 free novels and the surprise gift are mine to keep forever.   142-BPX-BP6S

Name _____ (PLEASE PRINT)

Address _____ Apt. No. _____

City _____ State/Prov. _____ Zip/Postal Code _____

This offer is limited to one order per household and not valid to present subscribers. Price is subject to change.   DOHT-SUB-1R

HARLEQUIN HISTORICAL

Explore love with Harlequin in the Middle Ages, the Renaissance, in the Regency, the Victorian and other eras.

Relive within these books the endless ages of romance, set against authentic historical backgrounds. Two new historical love stories published each month.

HIST-A-1